Everything You Need To Know To Take Care Of Your Pet Hamster

HAMTARO™
little hamsters big adventures

HAMSTER CARE GUIDE

Hamsters love to eat. They hold their food with their paws and—*Krmpkrmp!* As they eat, their cheeks puff with food.

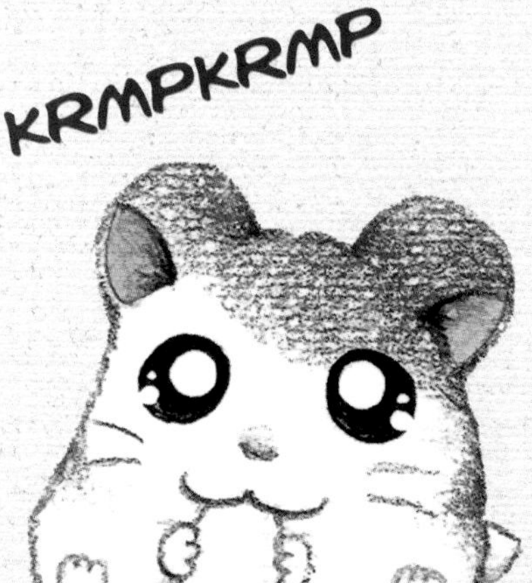
KRMPKRMP

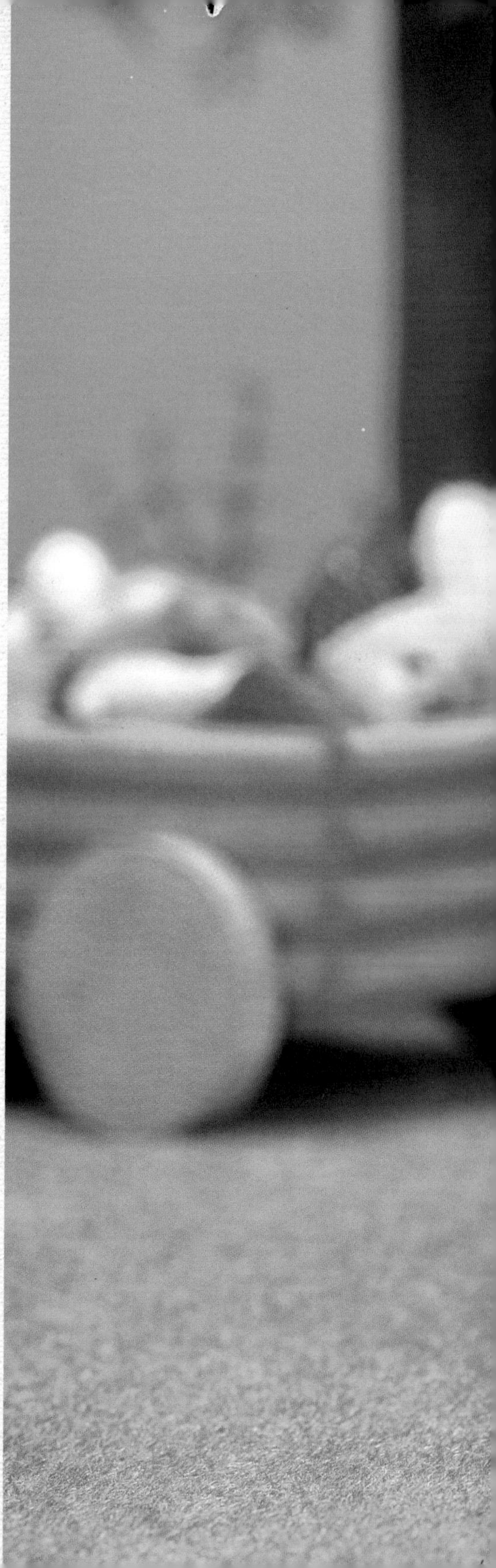

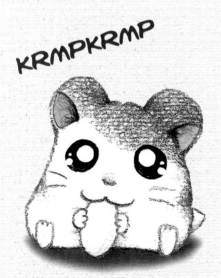

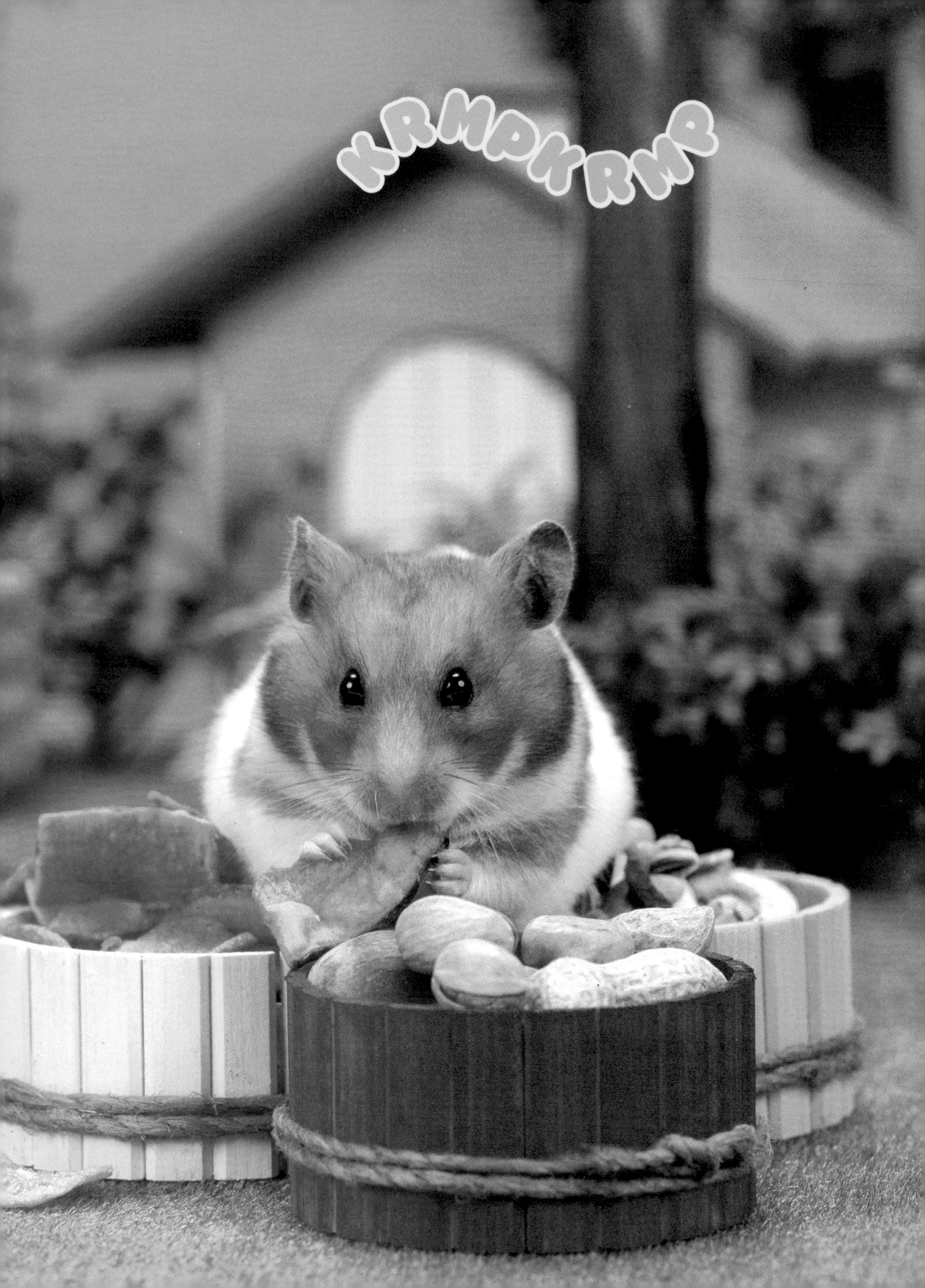
KRMPKRMP

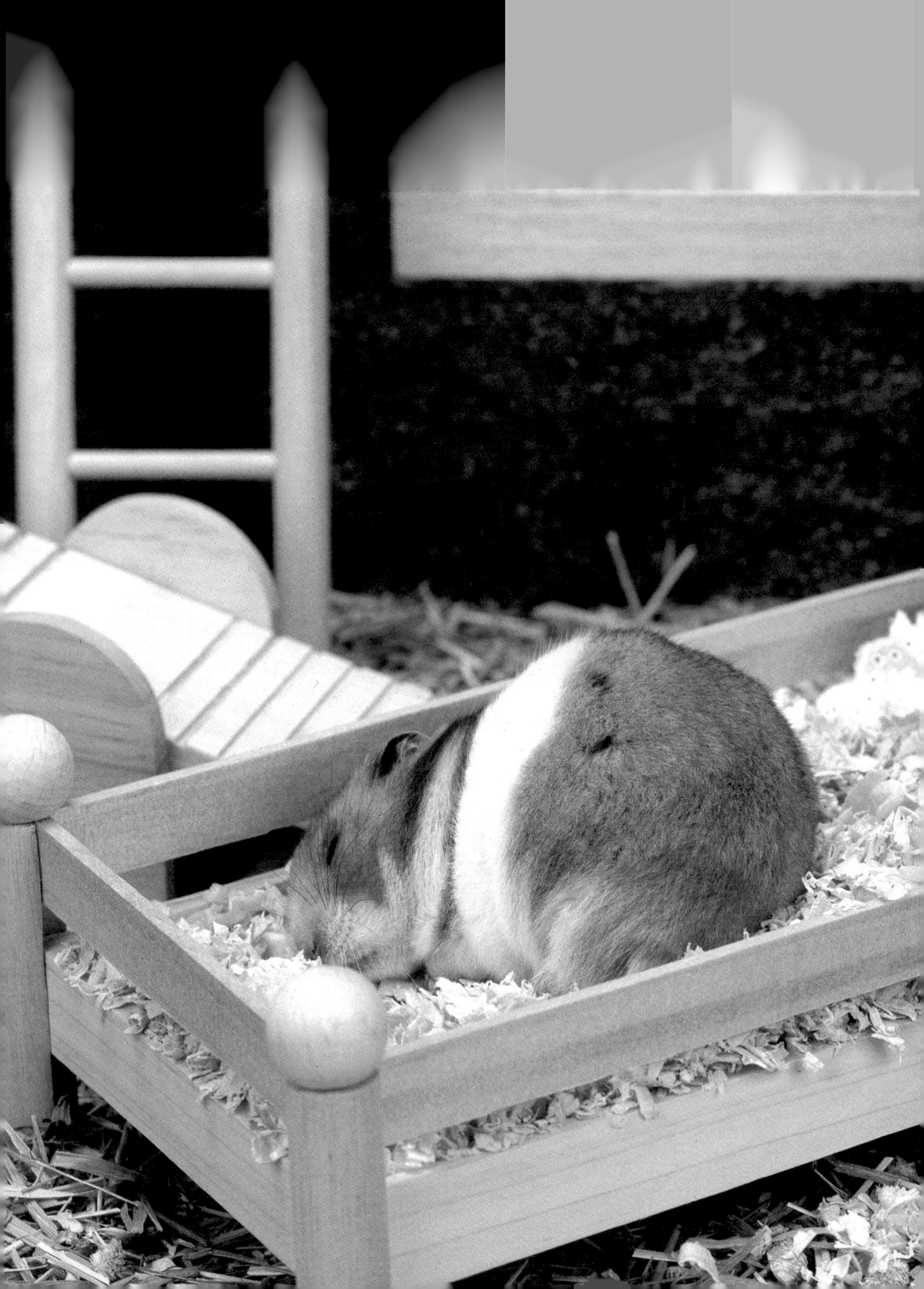

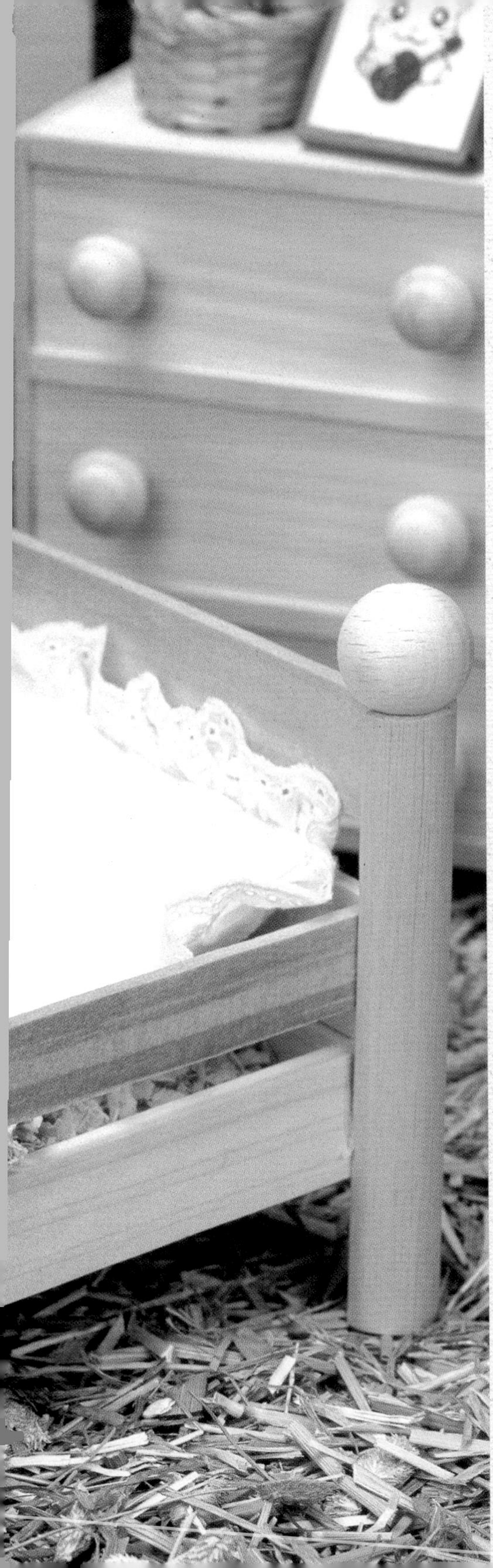

Hamsters love to sleep.
They roll up into a ball
and—*ZuZuZu*—
they are fast asleep.

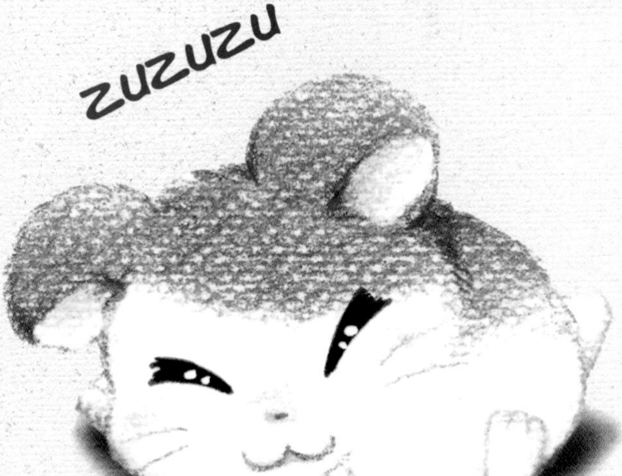
ZUZUZU

Hamsters love to look nice.
After waking up, they
begin to groom—
Kushi-Kushi!
They brush the hair on
their face and head.

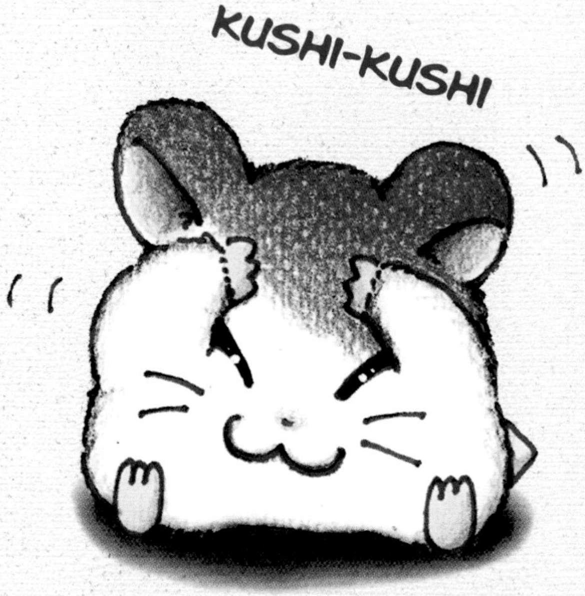
KUSHI-KUSHI

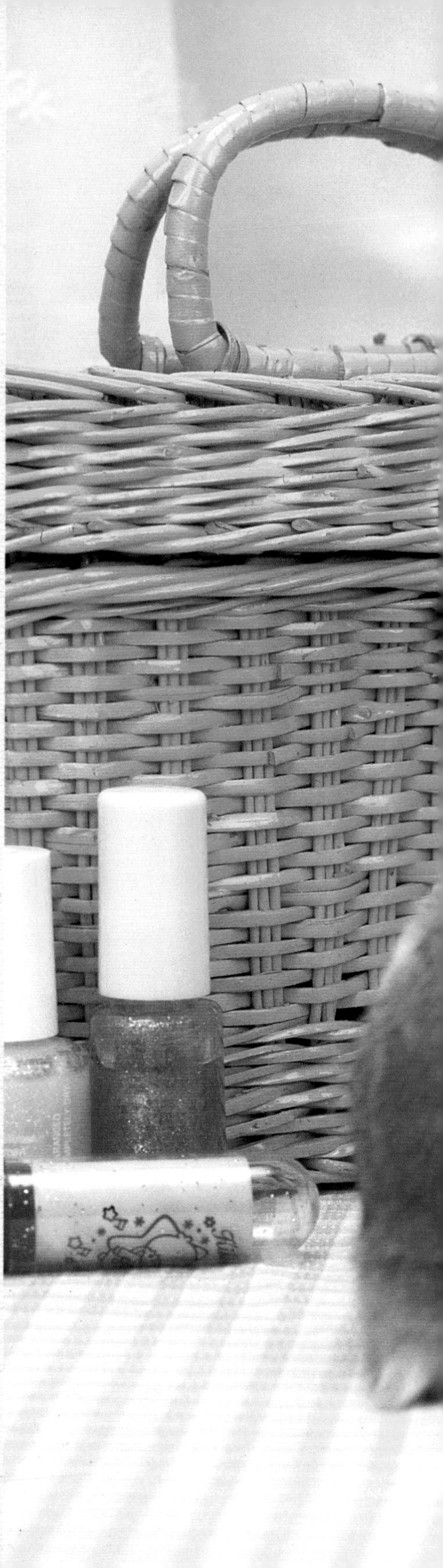

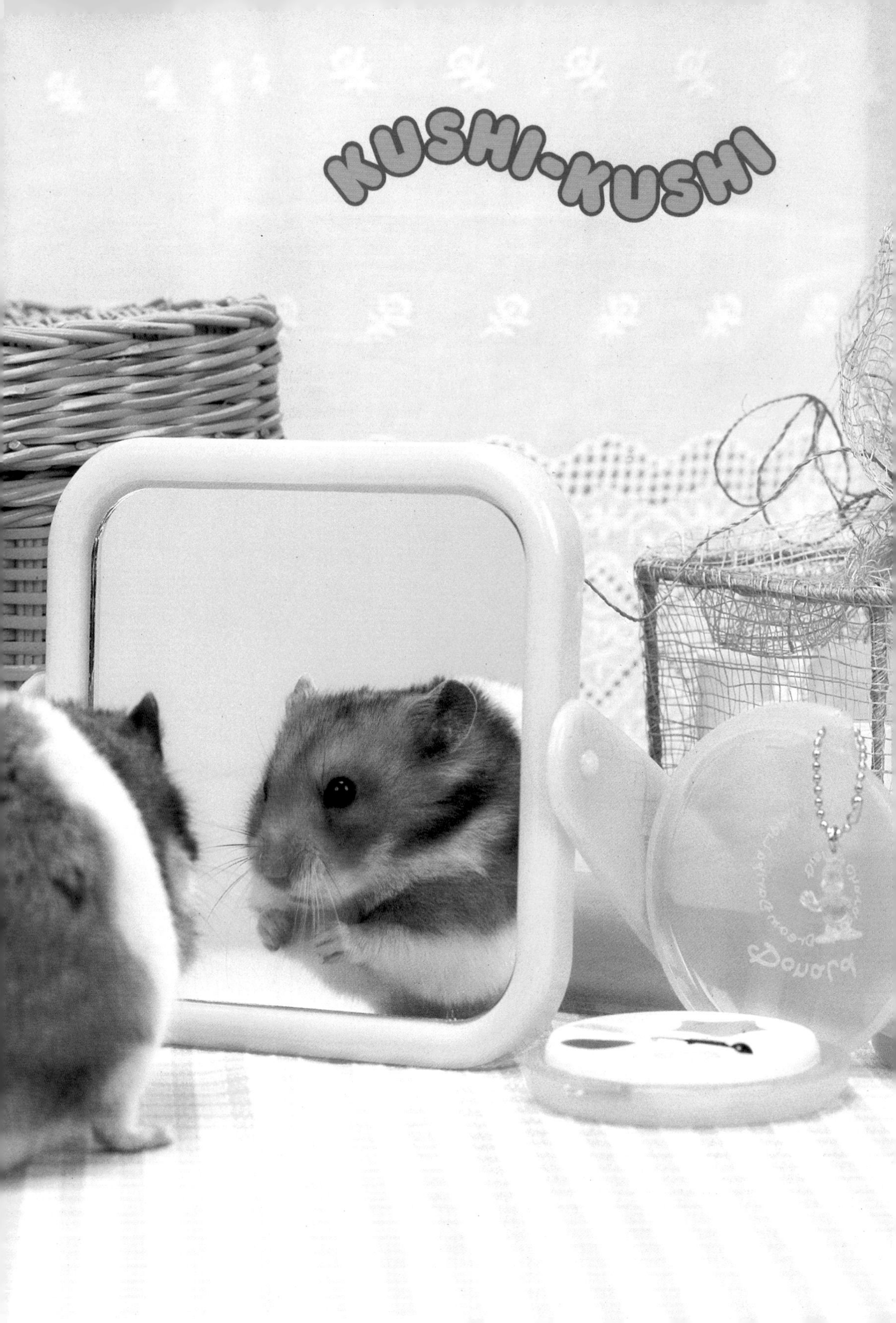
KUSHI-KUSHI

TABLE OF CONTENTS

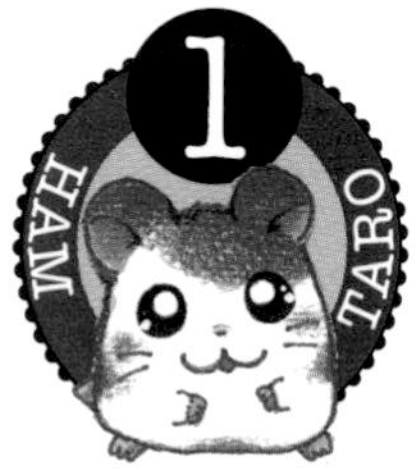
1
HAM
TARO

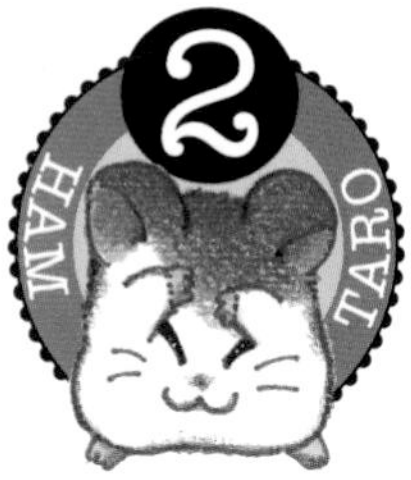
2
HAM
TARO

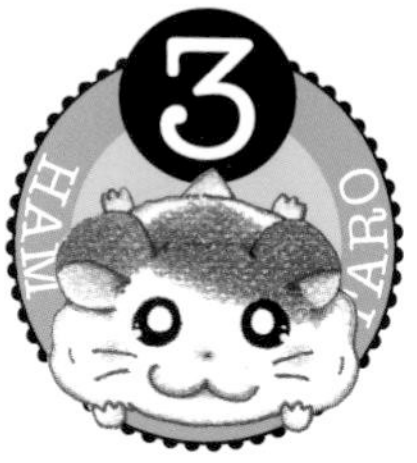
3
HAM

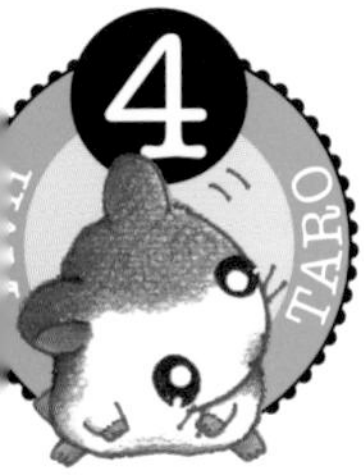
4
TARO

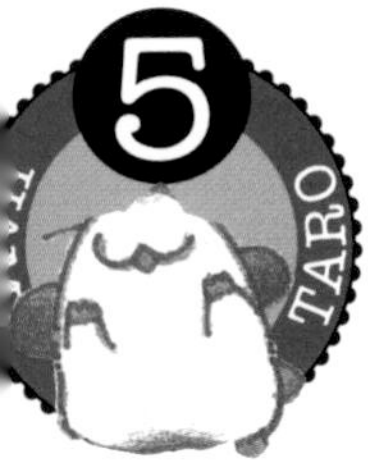
5
TARO

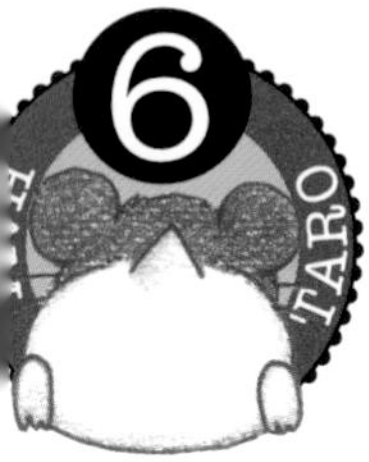
6
TARO

A REQUEST FROM YOUR HAMSTER

💙 Please take care of me every day.

🤍 Please be kind to me.

🤍 Please take care of me to the very end.

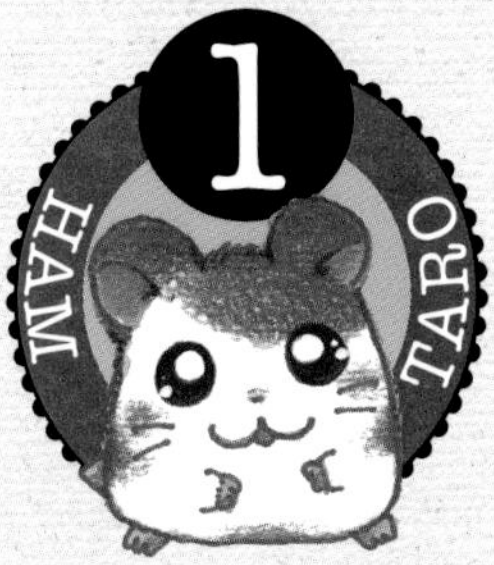
1
HAM
TARO

CHAPTER 1 • HAMSTER ENCYCLOPEDIA

**THERE ARE MANY DIFFERENT KINDS OF HAMSTERS.
PICK YOUR FAVORITE!**

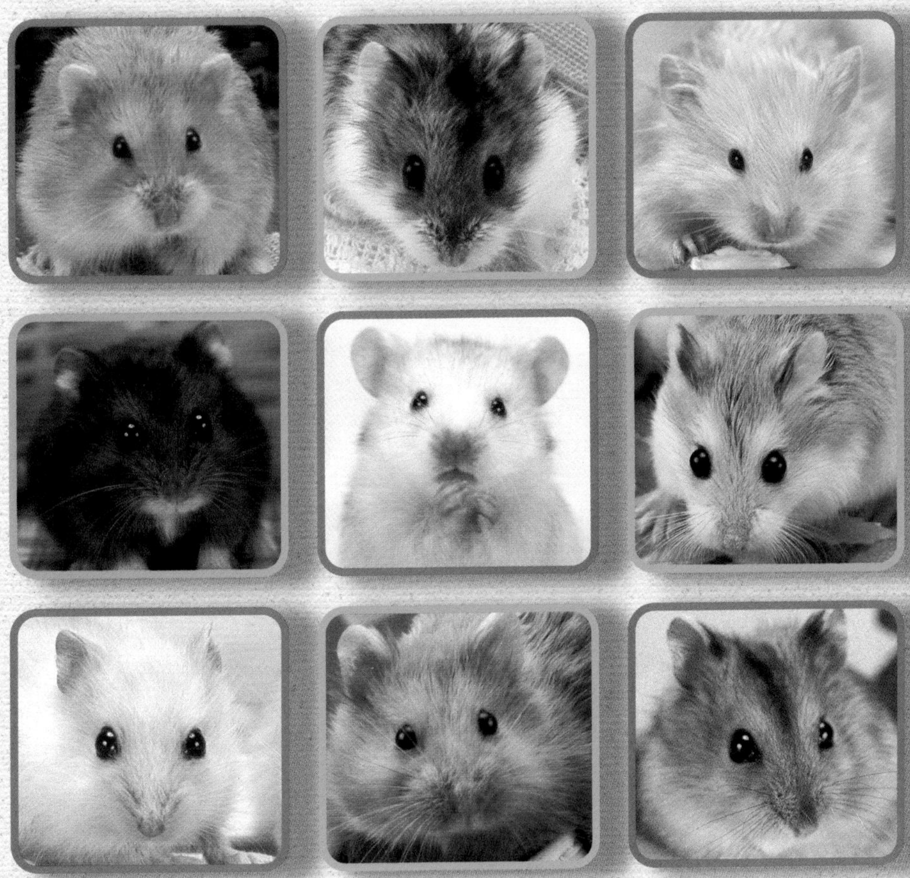

1
HAMSTER ENCYCLOPEDIA

GOLDEN HAMSTERS

Its body and cheek pouches are pretty big
Hamtaro is a Golden Hamster.

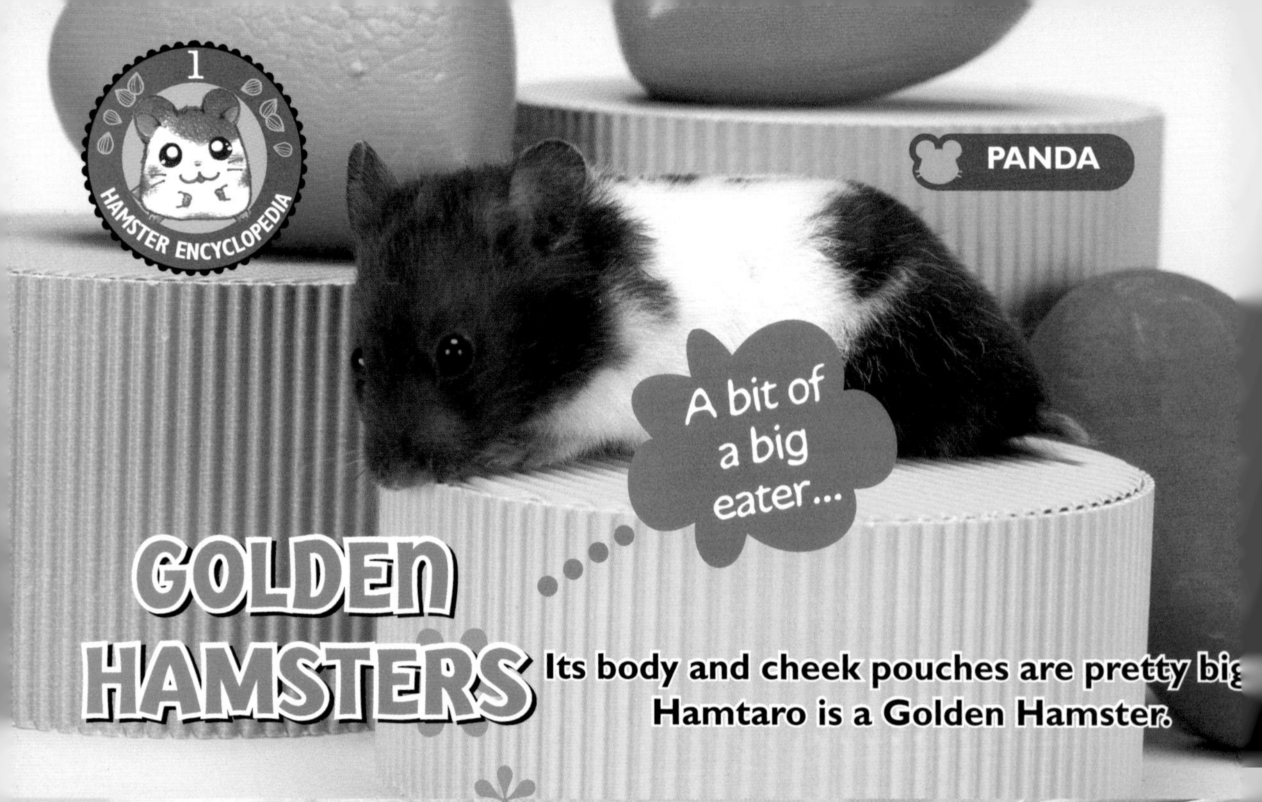
PANDA
A bit of a big eater...

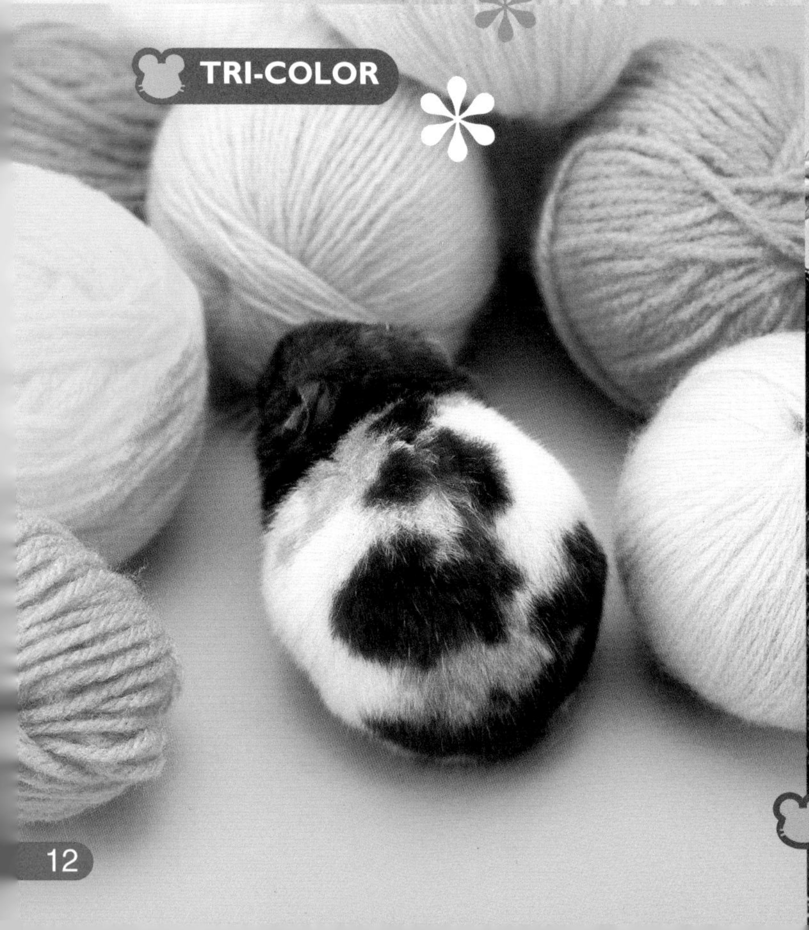
TRI-COLOR

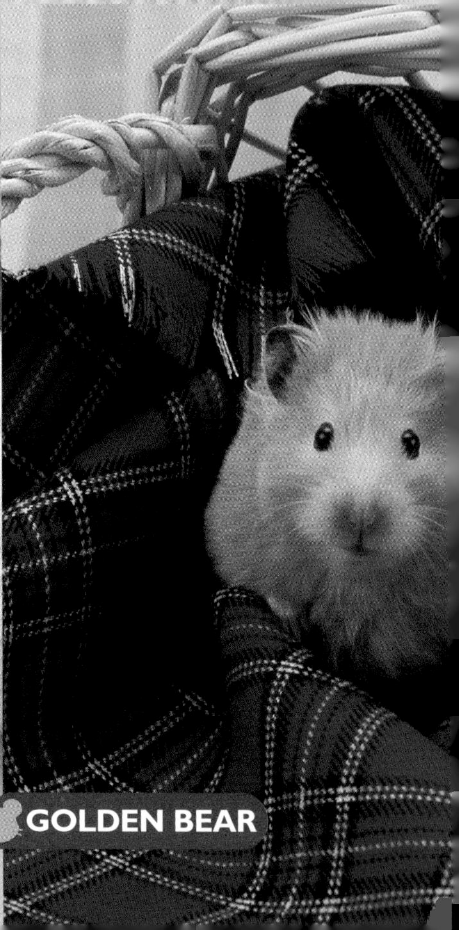
GOLDEN BEAR

NOTE

GOLDEN (SYRIAN) HAMSTERS

Weight: 3~7oz (80~210 gm)
Length: 7~8 in (12~19 cm)
Life Span: 1.5~3 years
Space required: 15 x 25 in (40 x 60 cm)
Babies per litter: 1~20

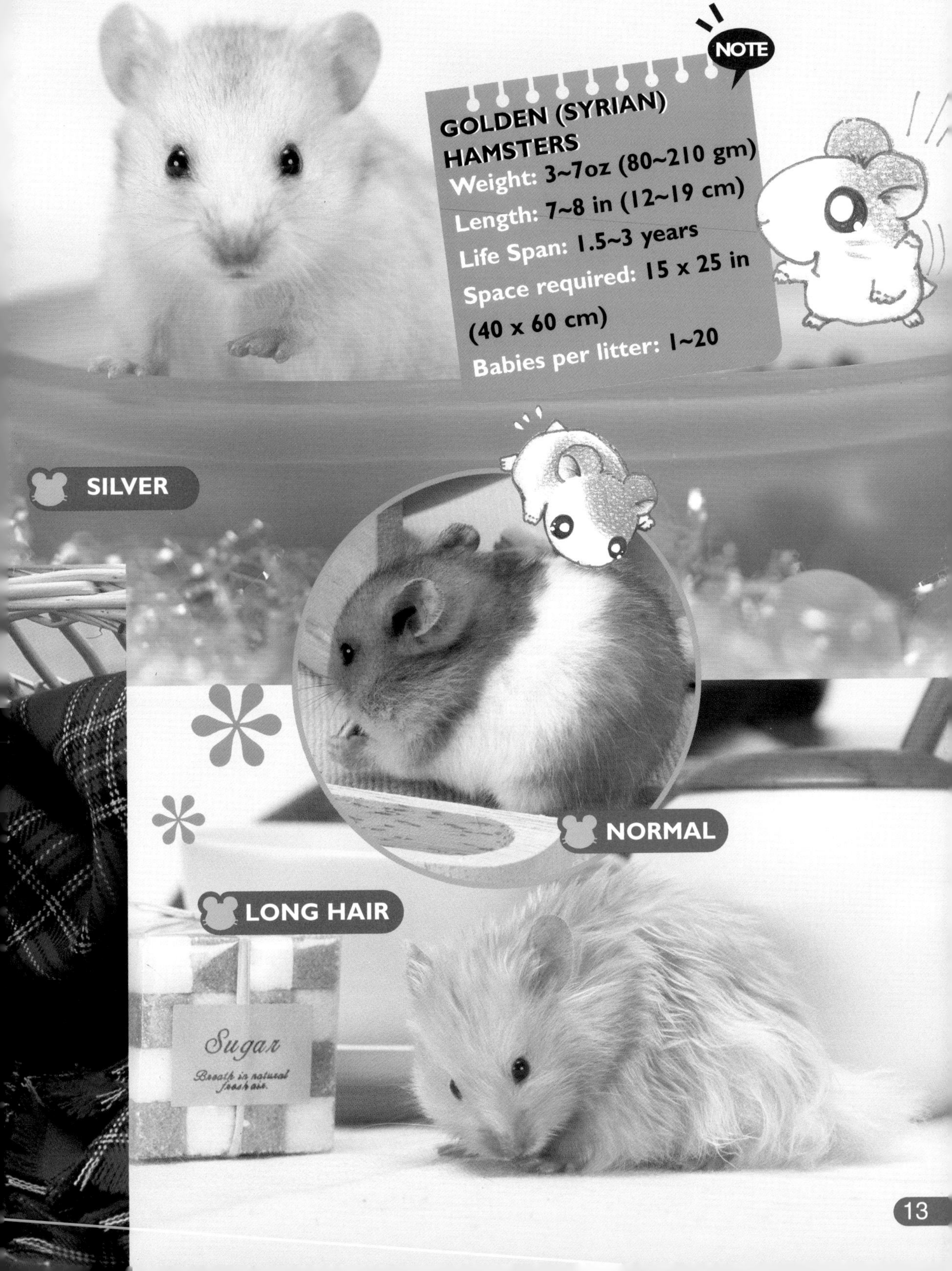
SILVER
NORMAL
LONG HAIR
Sugar
Breath in natural fresh air.

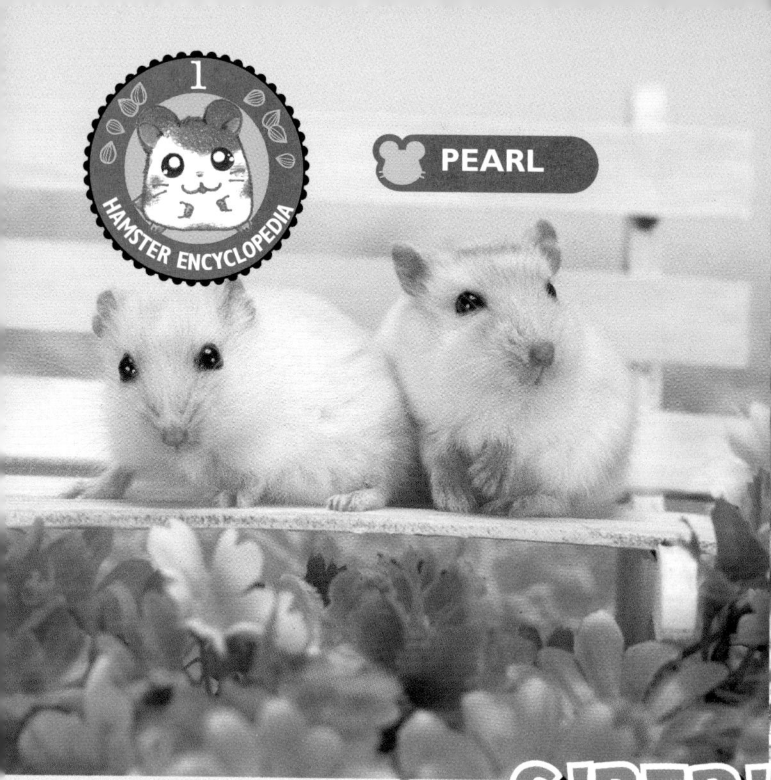
PEARL

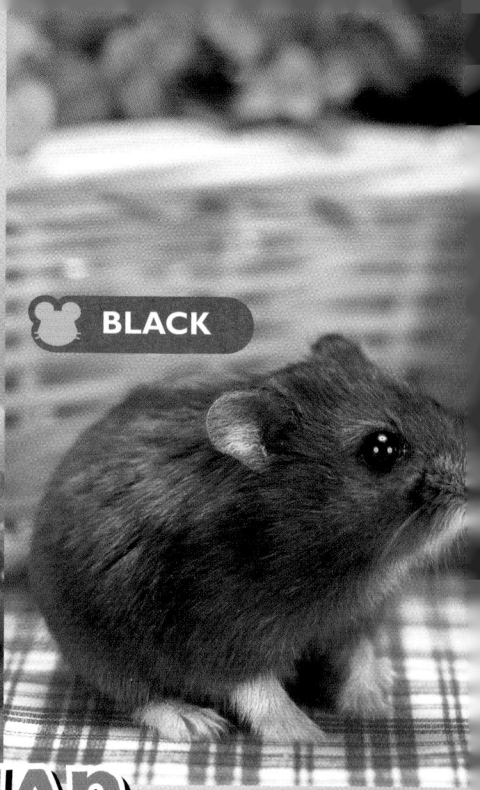
BLACK

A bit low-key...

SIBERIAN HAMSTERS

**A small, quiet, very sociable hamster.
It will quickly become your friend.**

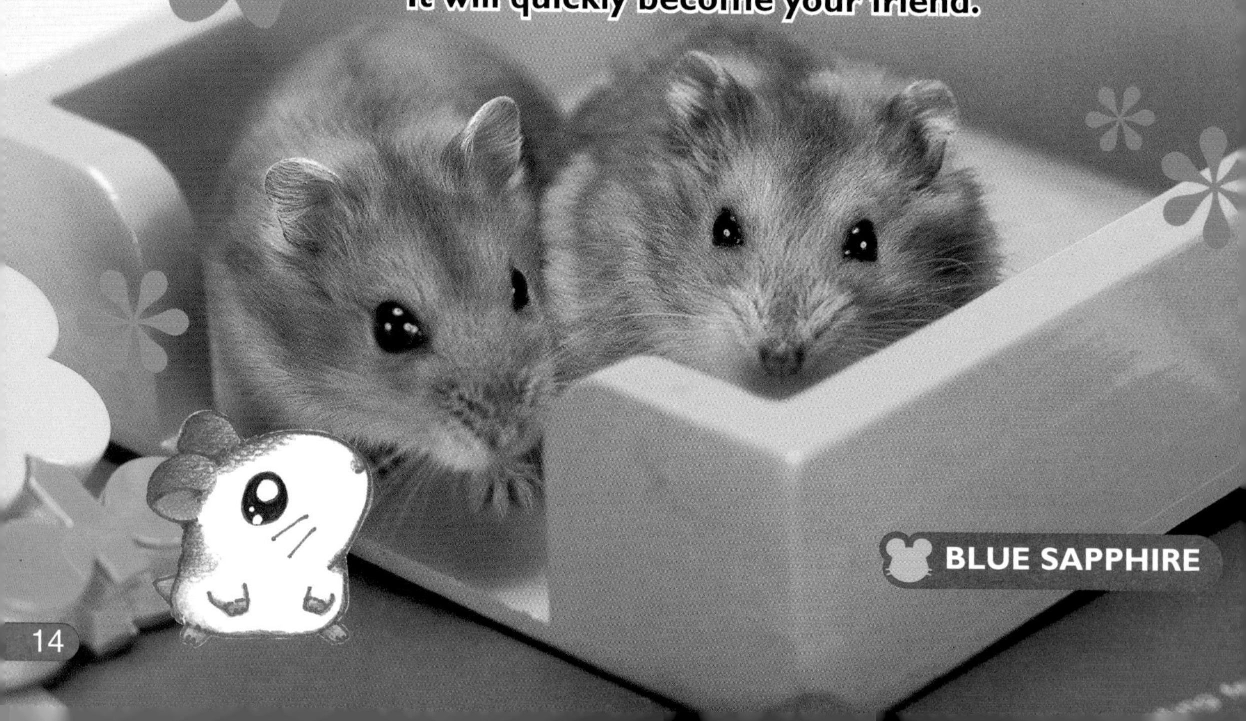
BLUE SAPPHIRE

NORMAL

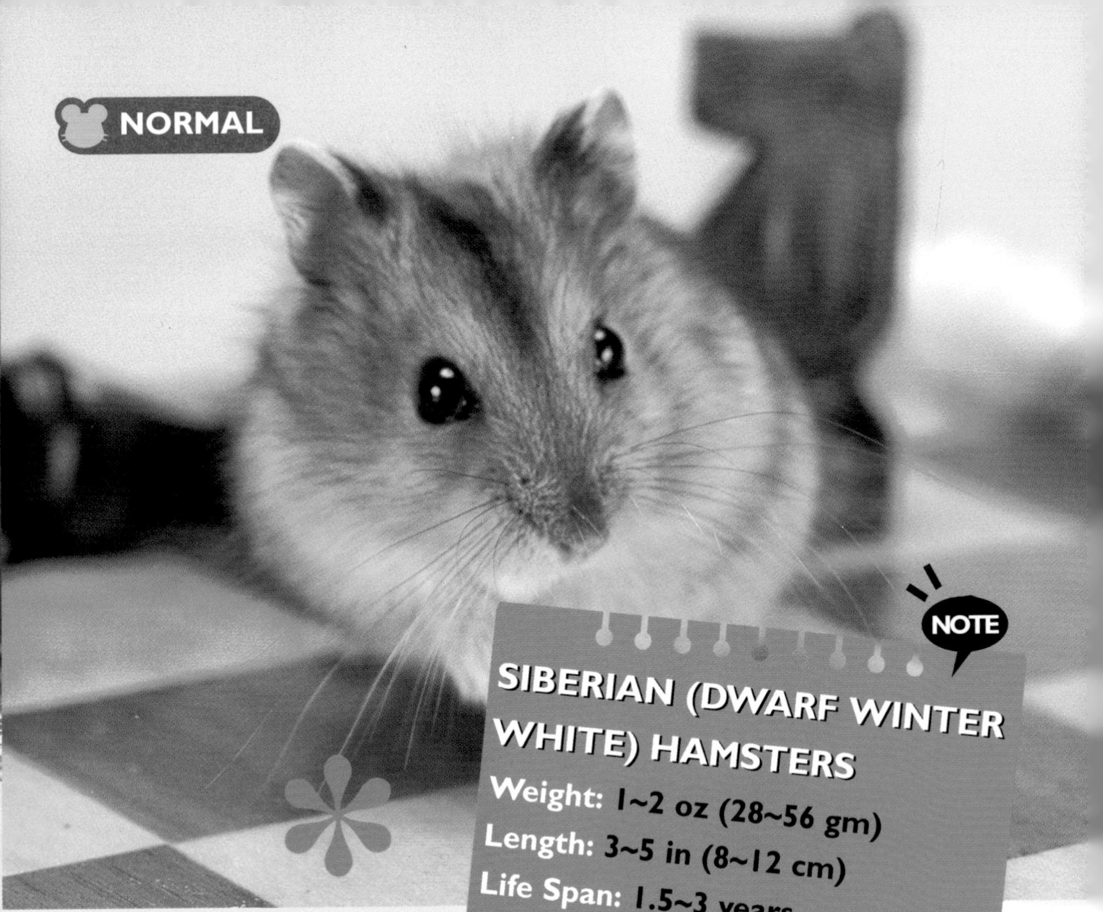

NOTE

SIBERIAN (DWARF WINTER WHITE) HAMSTERS

Weight: 1~2 oz (28~56 gm)
Length: 3~5 in (8~12 cm)
Life Span: 1.5~3 years
Living Space required:
About 12 x 16 in (30 x 40 cm)
Babies per litter: 4~6

PUDDING

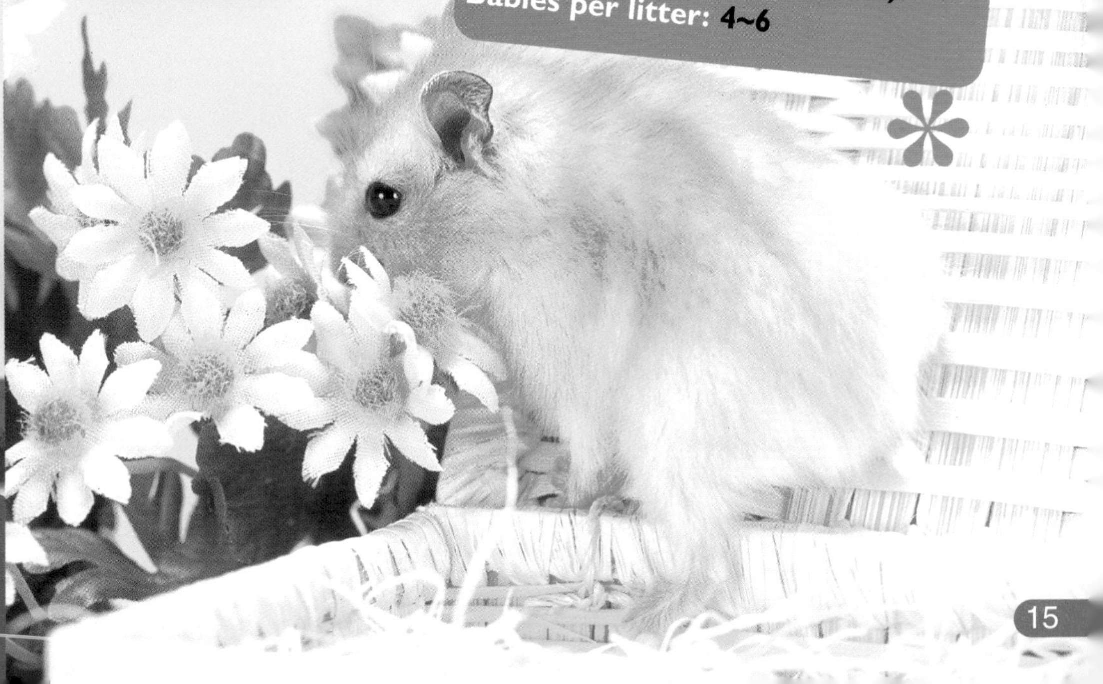

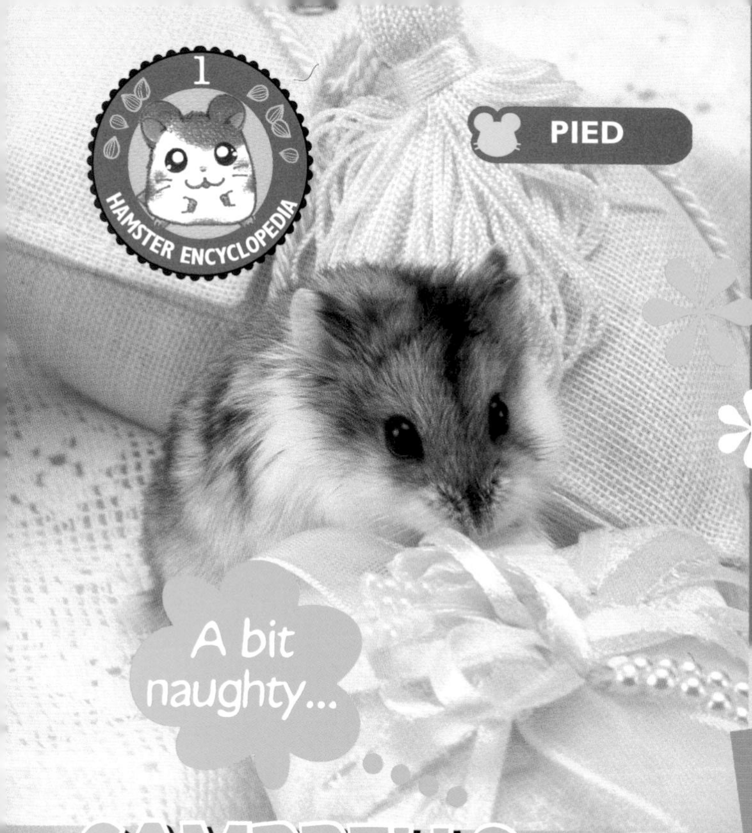
1
HAMSTER ENCYCLOPEDIA
PIED
A bit naughty...

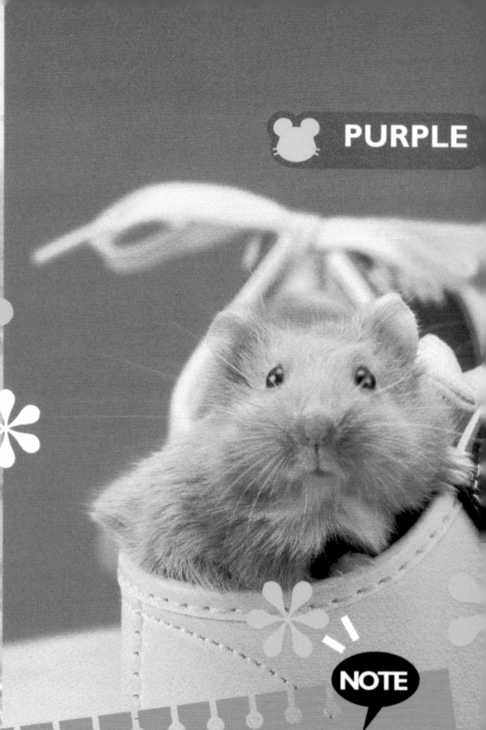
PURPLE

CAMPBELLS HAMSTERS

Although similar in size to the Siberian Hamster, Campbells Hamsters have strong-willed personalities.

NOTE

CAMPBELLS HAMSTERS

Weight: 1~1.7 oz (30~48 gm)

Length: 4~5 in (10~12 cm)

Life Span: 1.5~3

Space required:
About 12 x 16 in (30 x 40 cm)

Number of babies per litter:
About 1~9

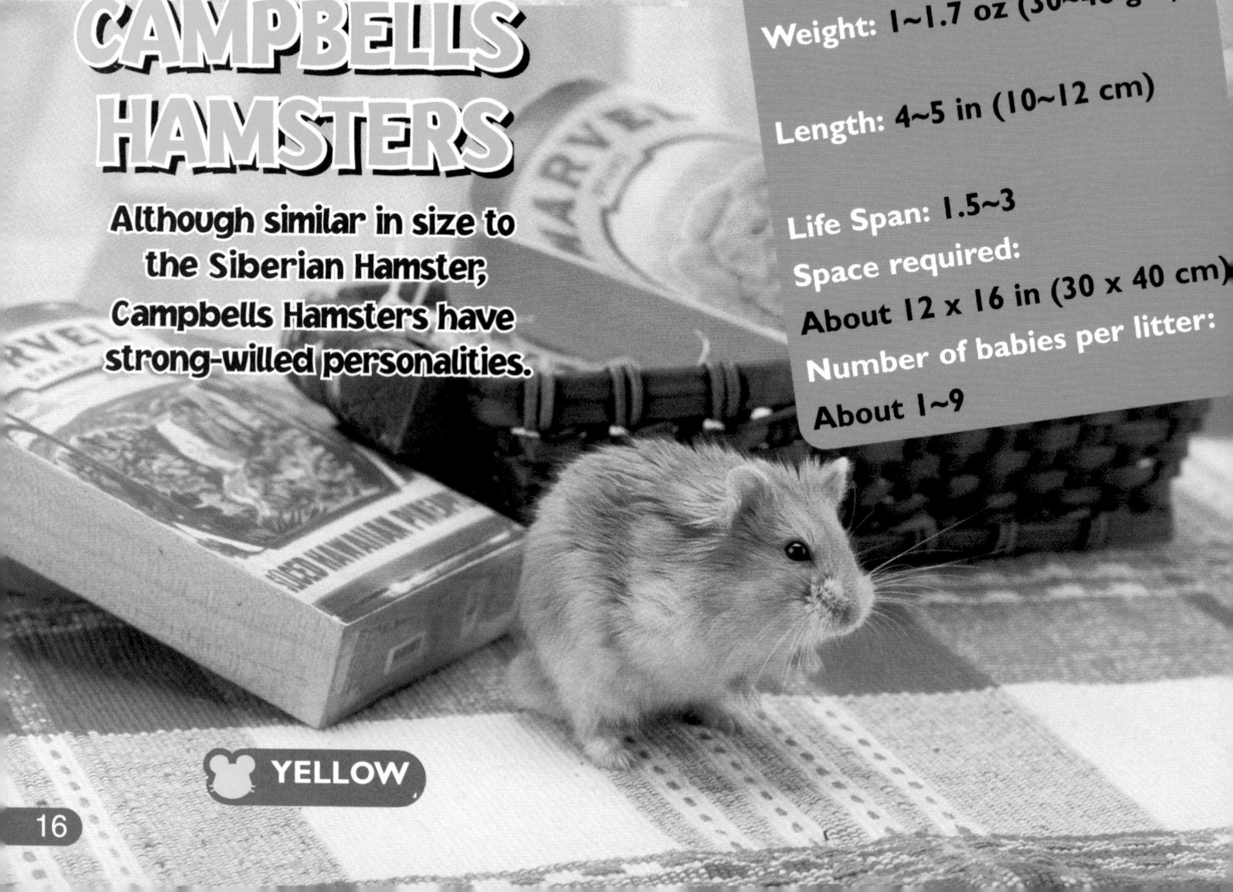
YELLOW

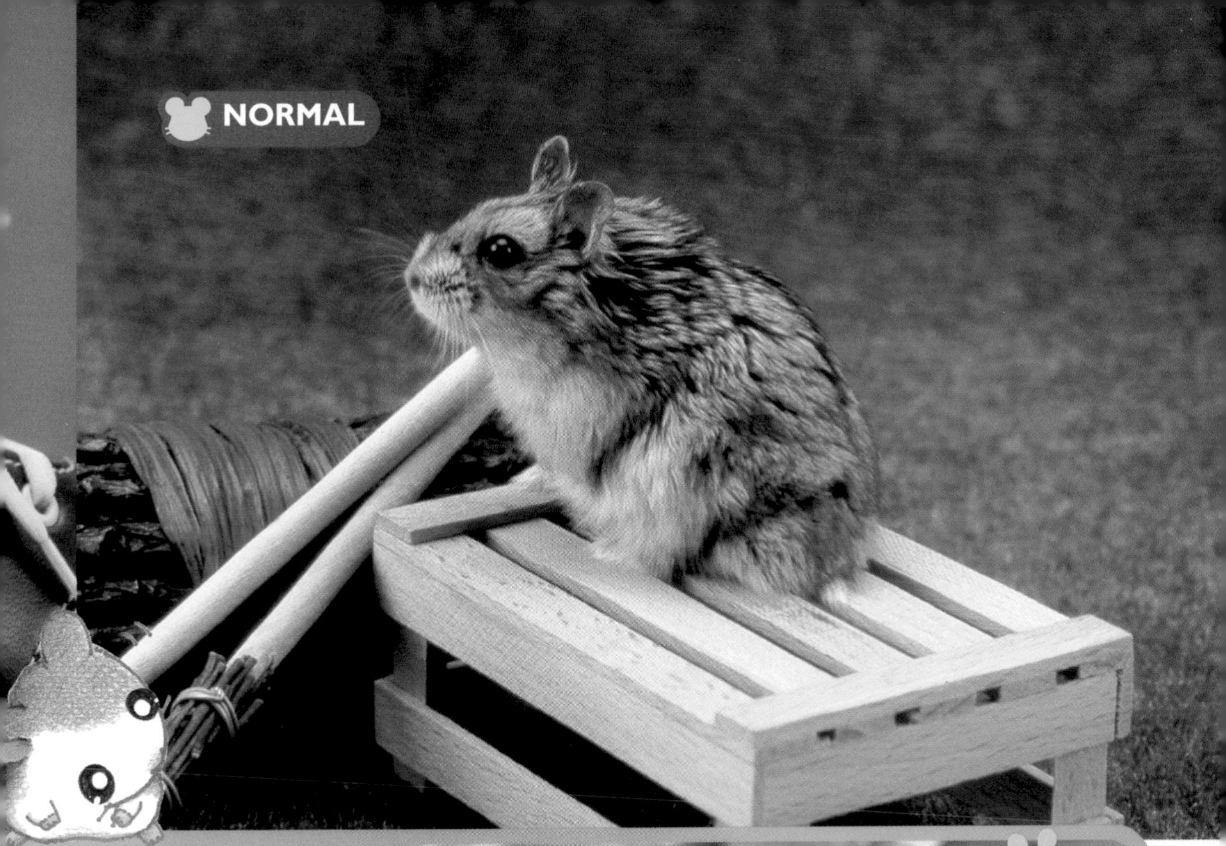
NORMAL

And the smallest...
ROBOROVSKI HAMSTERS

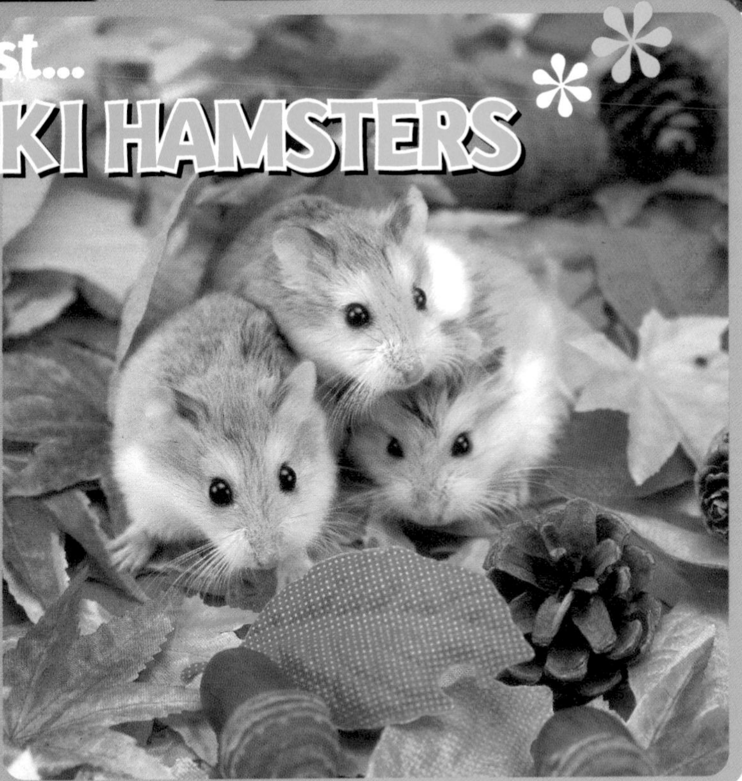

Female Roborovski Hamsters can be cared for in groups. They should be handled gently because they are so small.

NOTE

Weight: 1/2~3/4 oz (14~21 gm)
Length: 1.5~2 in (4~5 cm)
Life Span: About 3 years
Space required: About 12 x 16 in (30 x 40 cm)
Babies per litter: 1~6

TIPS ON HAMSTER SPECIES AND SELECTION

FOR STARTERS...

This book is intended to help parents and children learn about caring for hamsters together. Parents should oversee their child's efforts at hamster care, and lend a hand when necessary.
Animals don't always behave the way humans want them to. That is the difference between living things and mechanical toys or virtual pets. Hamsters need love, patience, and nurture, just like children.

VARIOUS SPECIES OF HAMSTERS

Related to the mouse family, hamsters originated in Eurasia. This chapter introduces hamsters that are readily available at the pet store.

GOLDEN HAMSTER

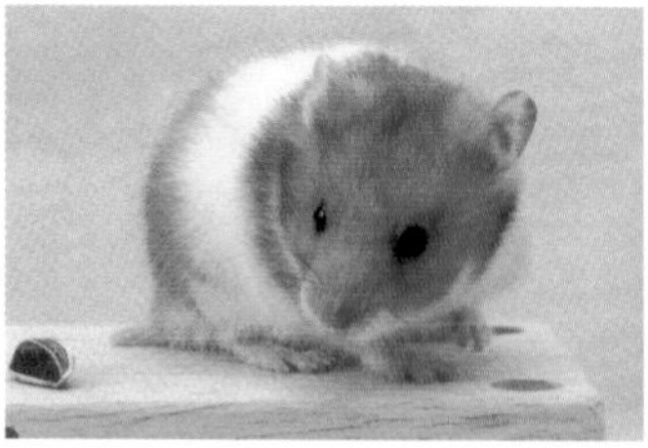

GOLDEN (SYRIAN) HAMSTERS

Because of its size, temperament, and willingness to be handled, the Golden Hamster is the easiest hamster for children to care for. Generally mild in personality, this hamster will become a very good friend if gently and frequently handled. This book uses the care of Golden Hamsters as the basic model.

SIBERIAN (DWARF WINTER WHITE) HAMSTERS

Siberian Hamsters usually become very close to humans and, as long as they are not handled roughly, rarely bite.

SIBERIAN HAMSTER

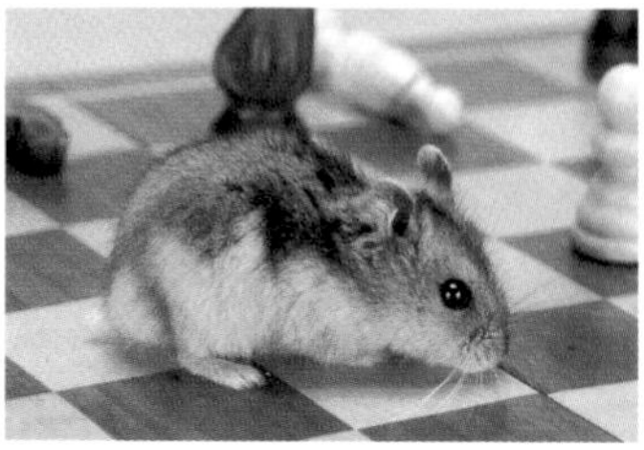

CAMPBELLS HAMSTERS

Because the Campbells Hamster is very territorial in nature, many will bite. However, if they are slowly introduced to handling and cared for gently, the Campbells Hamster can become friendly.
The former three types of hamsters must be kept one to a cage.

ROBOROVSKI HAMSTERS

As the smallest of the pet hamsters, the Roborovski Hamster is known for its cute appearance and behavior. As with the other small hamsters, this hamster must be handled very gently and carefully, if at all. Keeping a male and female together will result in overpopulation, and keeping just males together will result in fighting. If you want to keep several together, choose females.

PET STORE CHECKLIST

When buying a hamster, choose a healthy, active hamster. Since hamsters are night animals (nocturnal), they usually sleep during the day, which makes it hard to tell if a hamster is energetic and healthy. Visit the pet store in the late afternoon, if possible.
First, pick a pet store that is clean and where the workers know a lot about hamsters. When choosing a hamster, make sure to check for the following:

- It is energetic and has a good appetite.
- It does not have a mucus discharge from its eyes.
- Its bottom is not dirty or wet.
- Its teeth are aligned.
- It does not have discharge from its nose.
- Its fur is thick and healthy.
- When buying a male and female for breeding, make sure that they are not siblings.

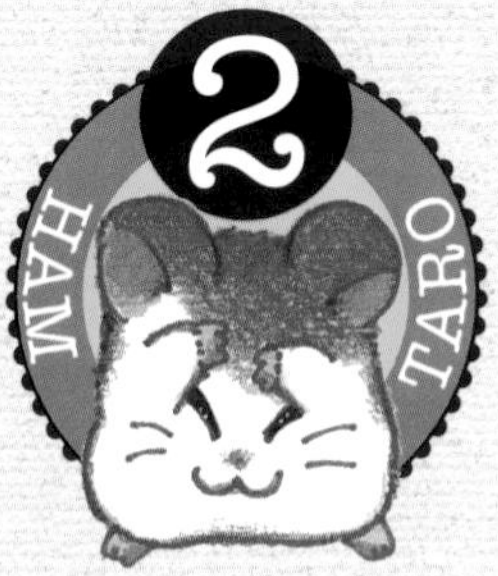
2
HAM
TARO

CHAPTER 2 • A HAMSTER'S HOME

A HAMSTER NEEDS A CLEAN, COMFORTABLE HOME TO BE HAPPY.

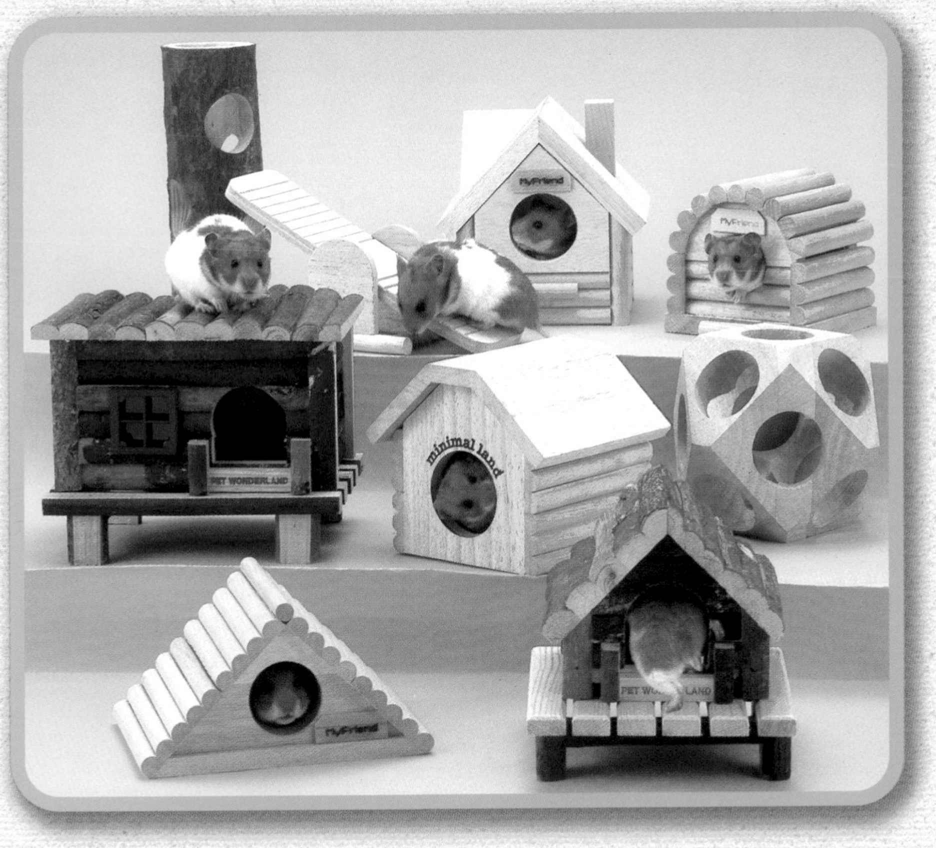
MyFriend
MyFriend
PET WONDERLAND
minimal land
MyFriend

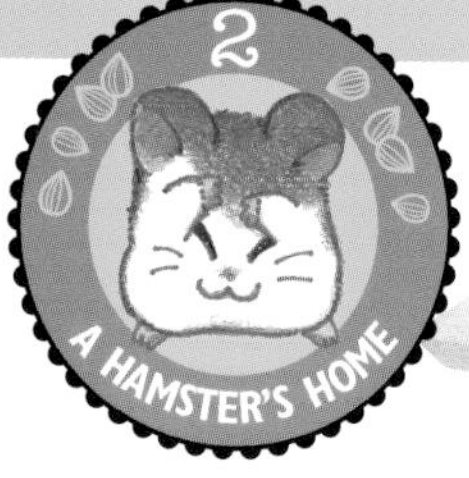
2
A HAMSTER'S HOME

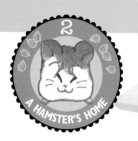

SOME NECESSARY EQUIPMENT FOR OWNING A HAMSTER.

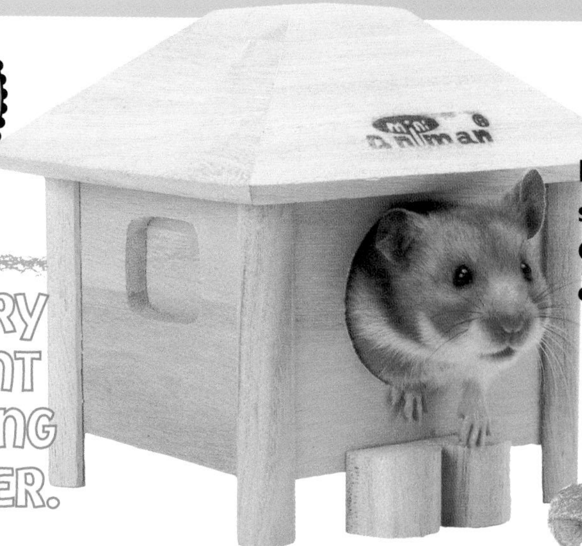

1 A LIVING ROOM (HAMSTER HOUSE

Hamsters like to sleep in dark places. Choose a house with fev openings and windows.

HOME SWEET HOME!

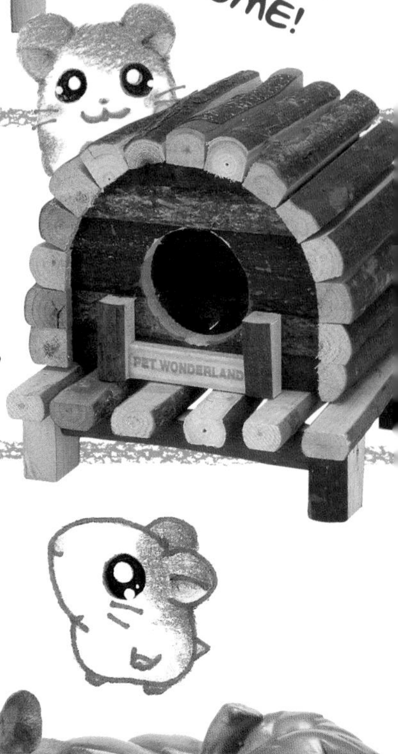

CHOOSING FURNITURE FOR YOUR HAMSTER.

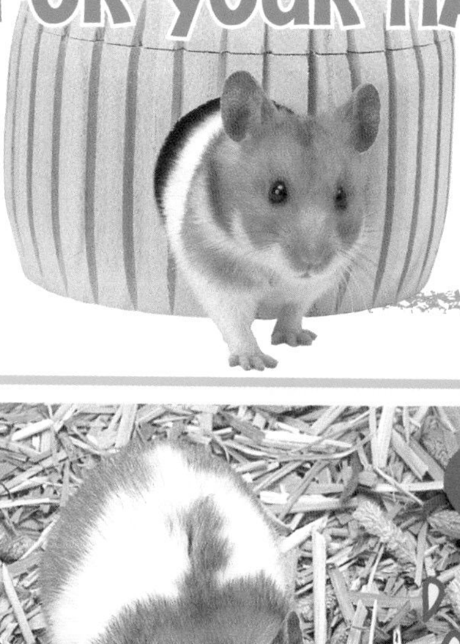

So your hamster can live a happy and comfortable life, assemble some simple furniture.

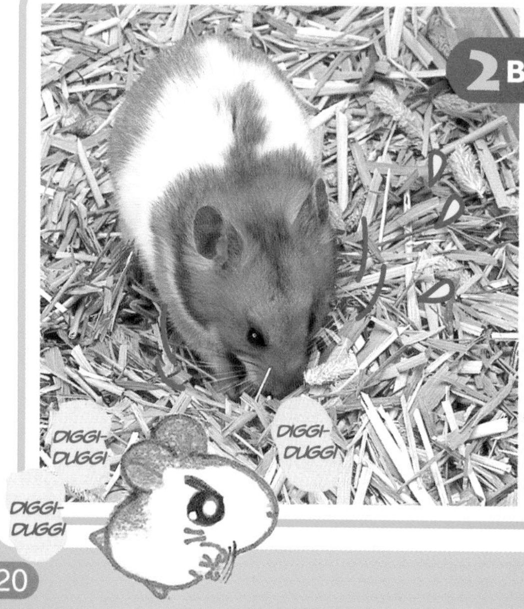
DIGGI-DUGGI
DIGGI-DUGGI
DIGGI-DUGGI

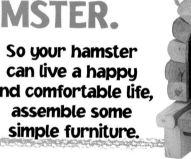

2 BEDDING

Use a pet store bedding of corncob, paper, or woodchips. Do not use cotton or cedar chips because these may harm your hamster.

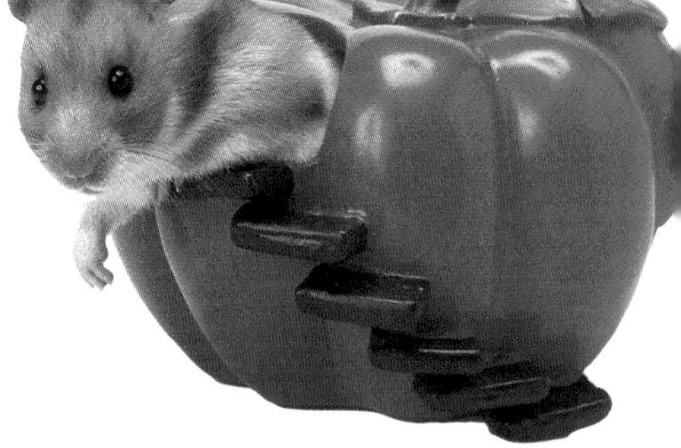

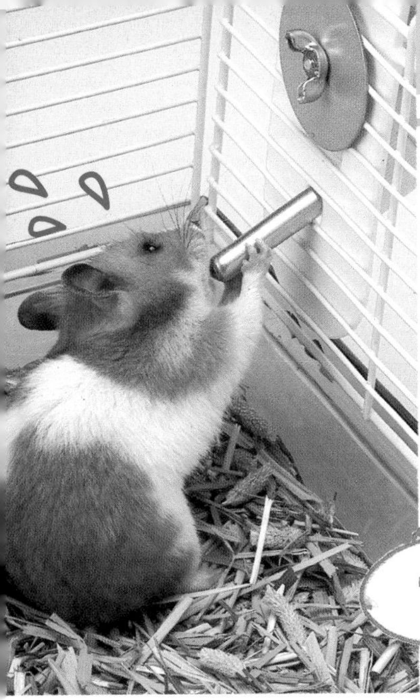

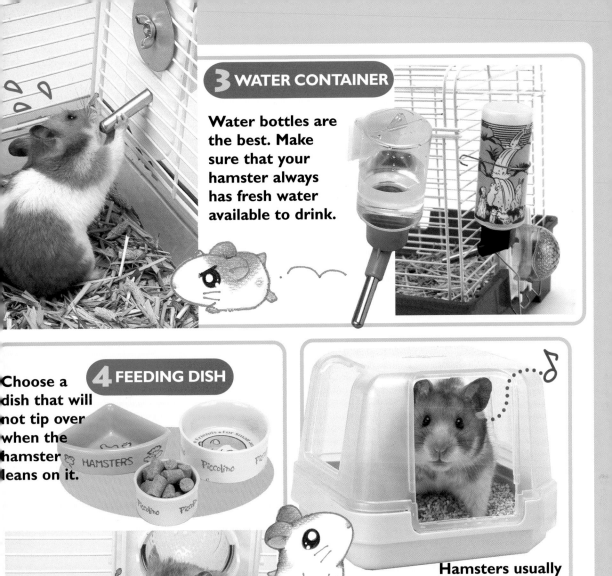

3 WATER CONTAINER

Water bottles are the best. Make sure that your hamster always has fresh water available to drink.

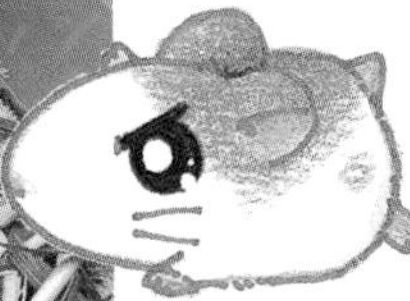

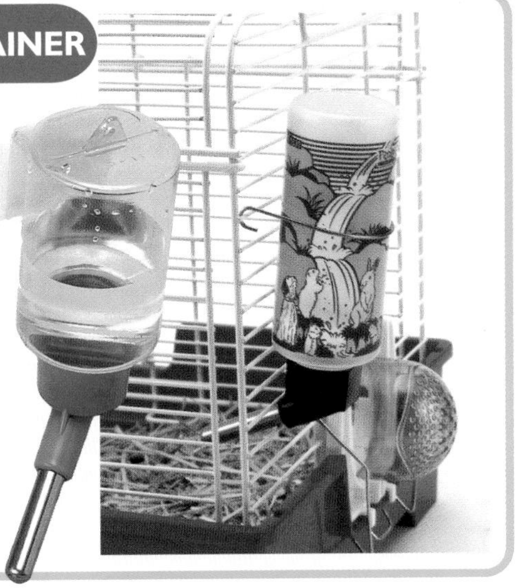

4 FEEDING DISH

Choose a dish that will not tip over when the hamster leans on it.

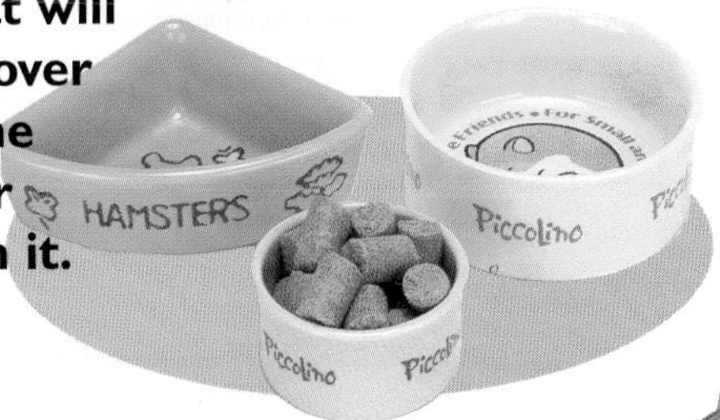
HAMSTERS
Piccolino
Piccolino

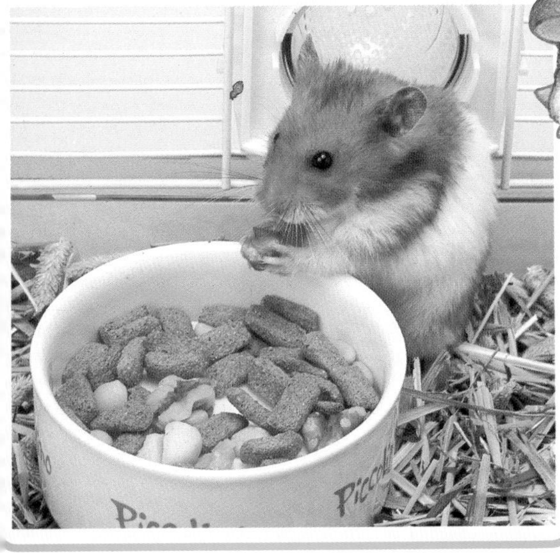

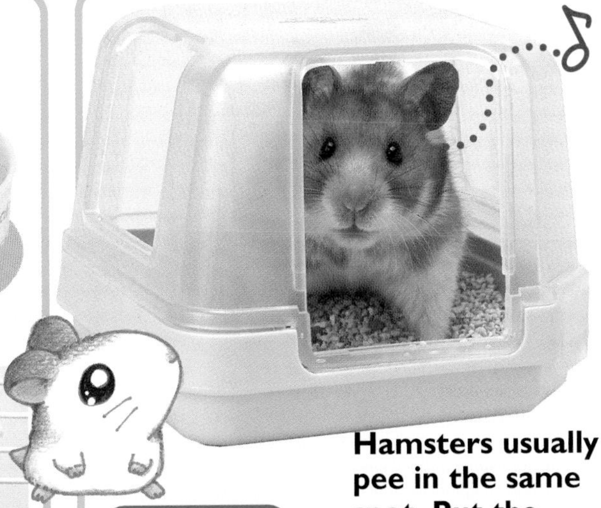

5 POTTY

Hamsters usually pee in the same spot. Put the potty with hamster litter in that location. They will make droppings anywhere, so be sure to clean them up!

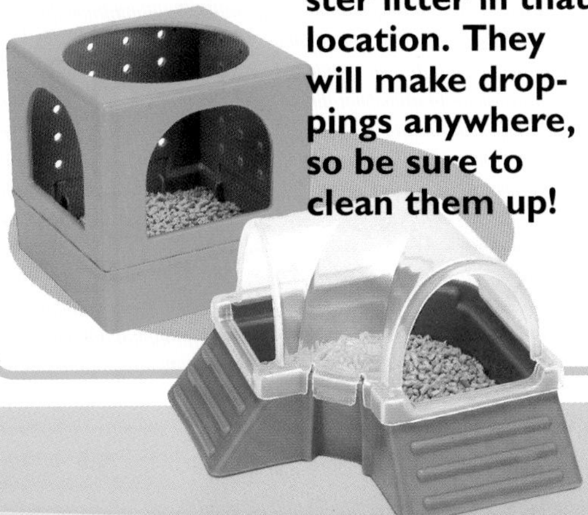

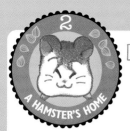

PLAYTHINGS THAT YOUR HAMSTER WILL LOVE.

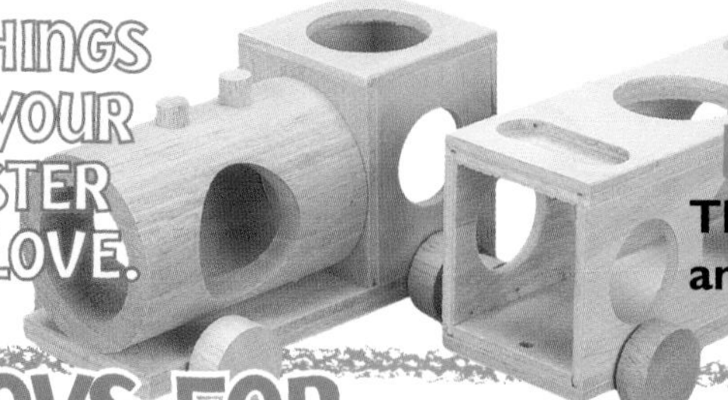

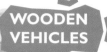

WOODEN VEHICLES

They like to get on and off–very busy!

SELECTING TOYS FOR YOUR HAMSTER.

Hamsters love to play alone. Select fun and safe toys for them to play with.

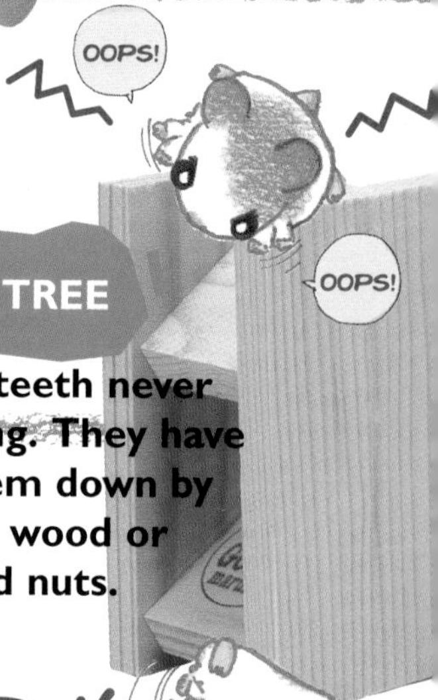
OOPS!
OOPS!

CHEW TREE

Hamsters' teeth never stop growing. They have to wear them down by gnawing on wood or hard-shelled nuts.

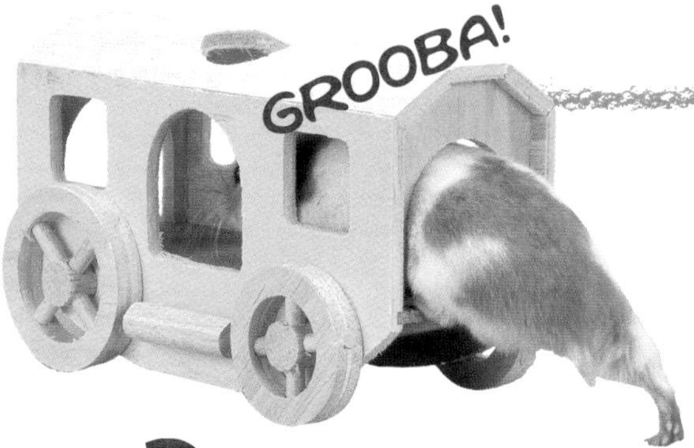
GROOBA!

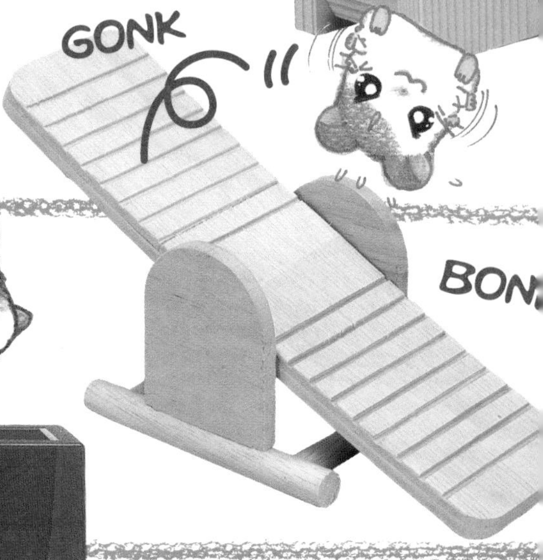
GONK
BON

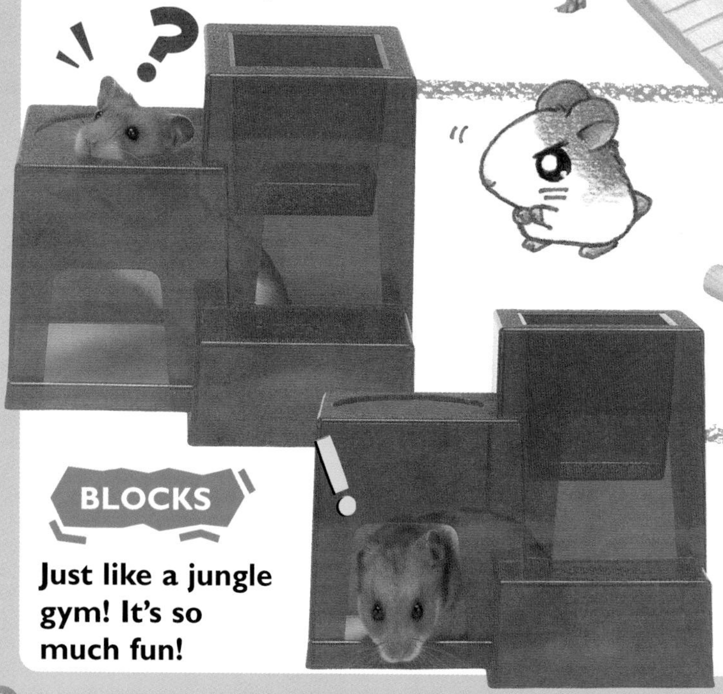

BLOCKS

Just like a jungle gym! It's so much fun!

SEESAW

Going up an going down Gonk! Bonk!

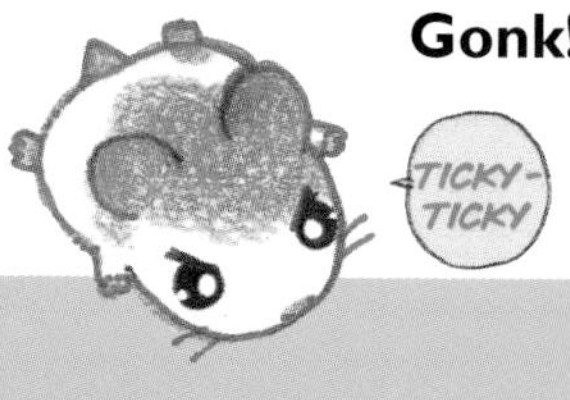
TICKY-TICKY

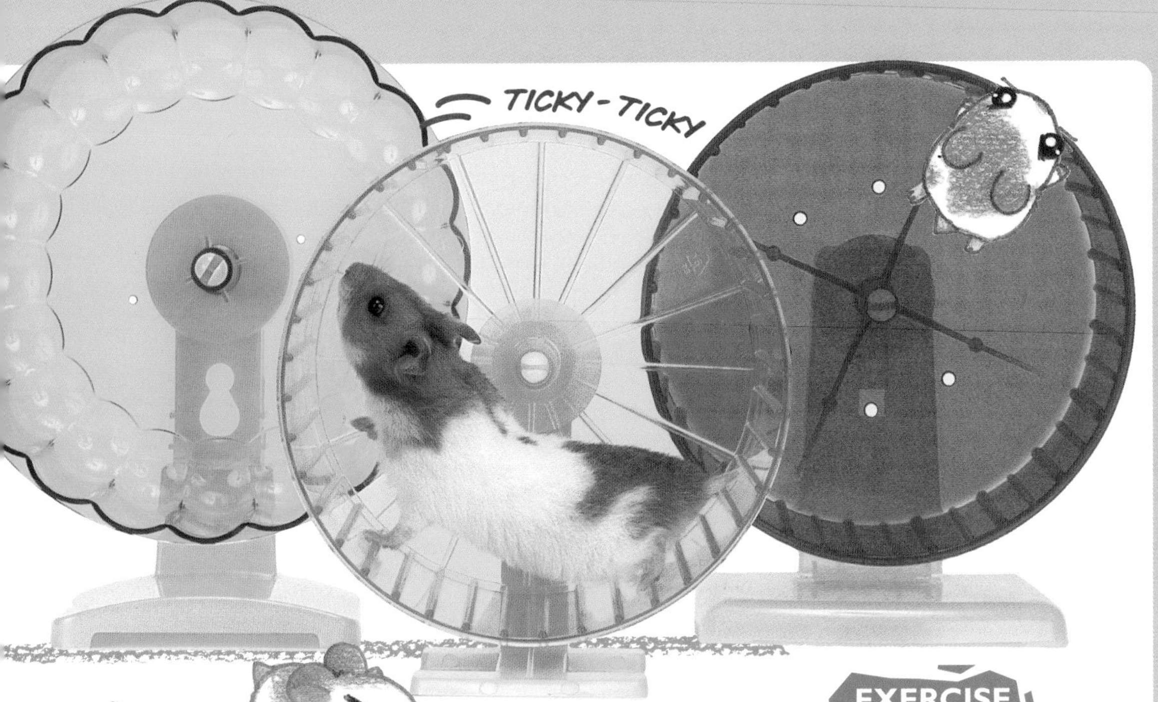
TICKY-TICKY

EXERCISE WHEEL

Hamsters need exercise. They enjoy running in a wheel.

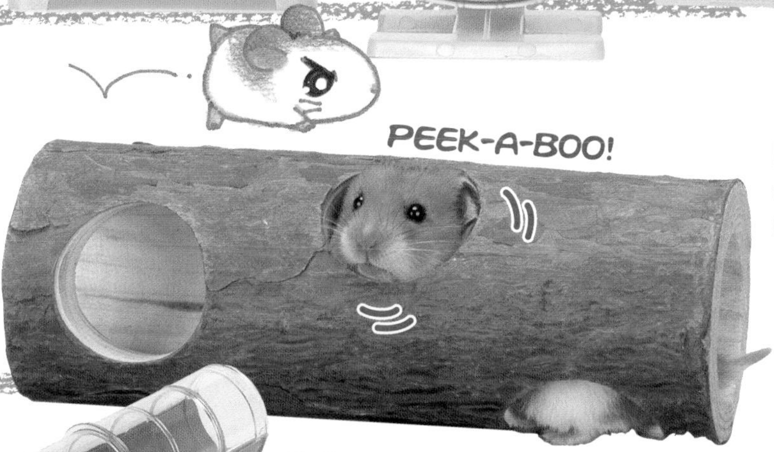
PEEK-A-BOO!

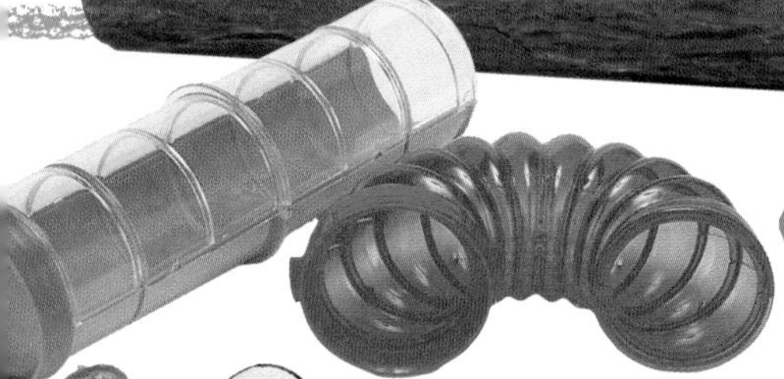

TUBE

Hamsters love to squeeze into tight places.

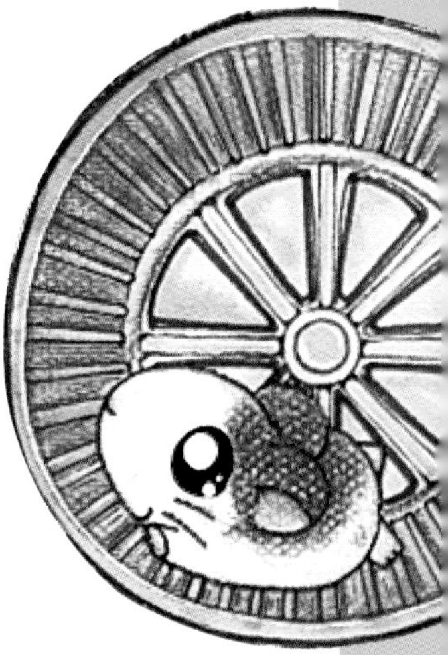

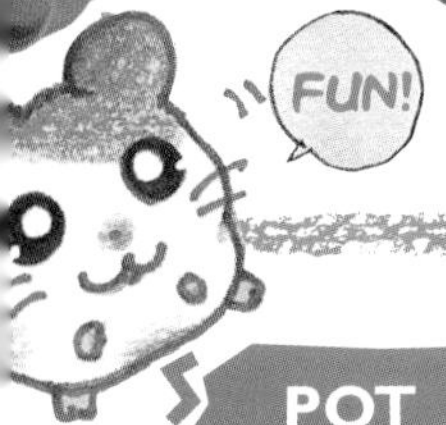
FUN!

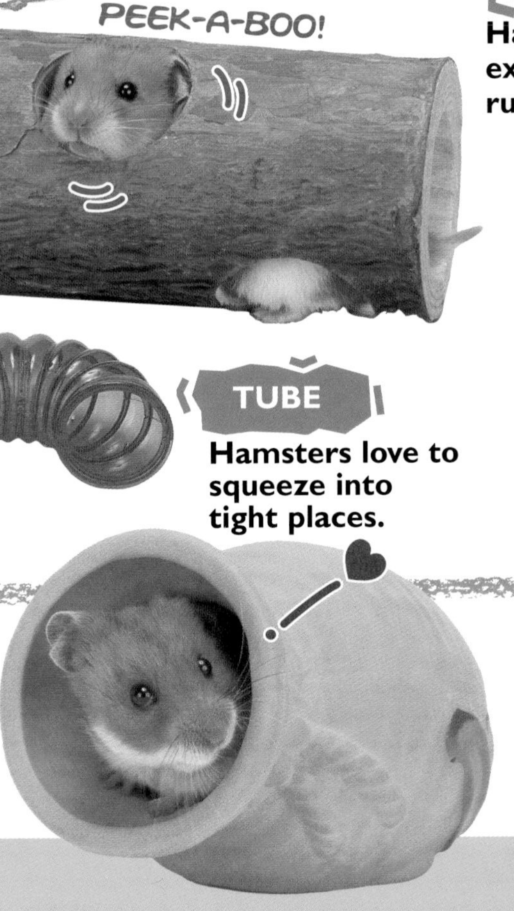

POT

They also like to crawl into dark spaces and dig around.

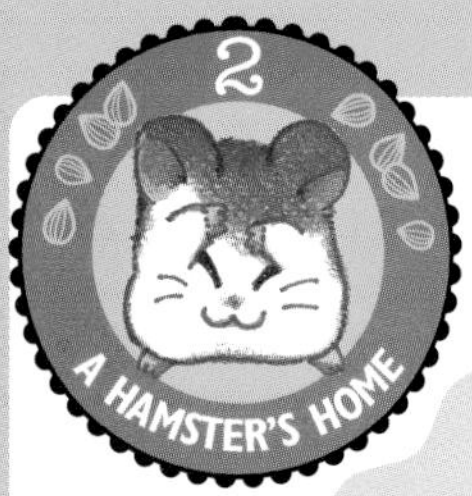
2
A HAMSTER'S HOME

HOW TO PLACE THE FURNITURE IN A COMFORTABLE LAYOUT.

MAKING A HOME FOR YOUR HAMSTER.

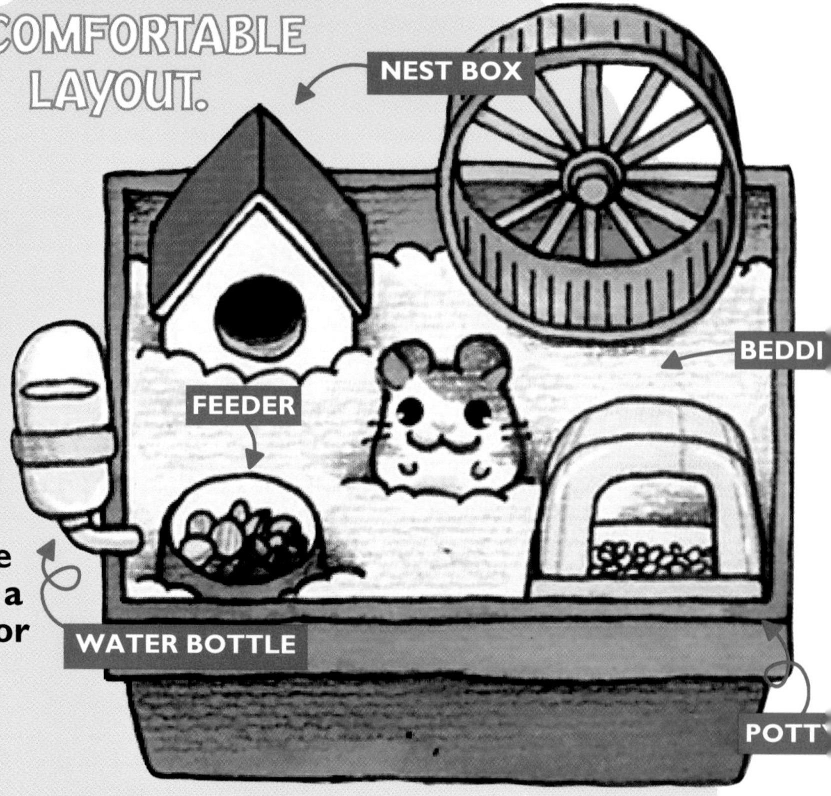
NEST BOX
BEDDI
FEEDER
WATER BOTTLE
POTT

Arrange furniture and toys to make a wonderful home for your hamster.

Layout from Above

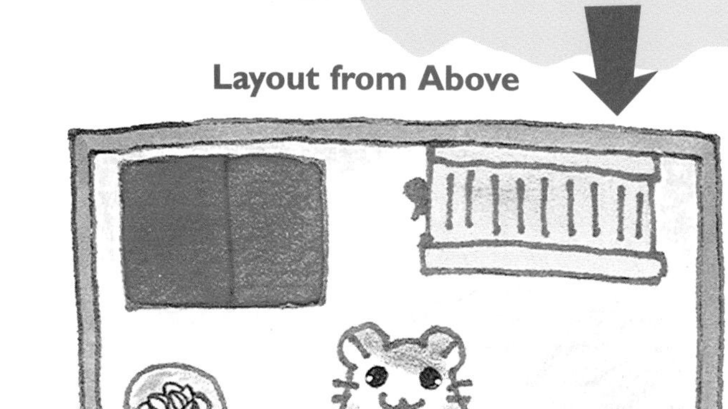

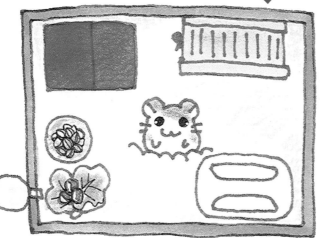

Placing its home and potty in the corners of a cage will comfort your hamster. Make sure the water bottle is easy for your hamster to reach.

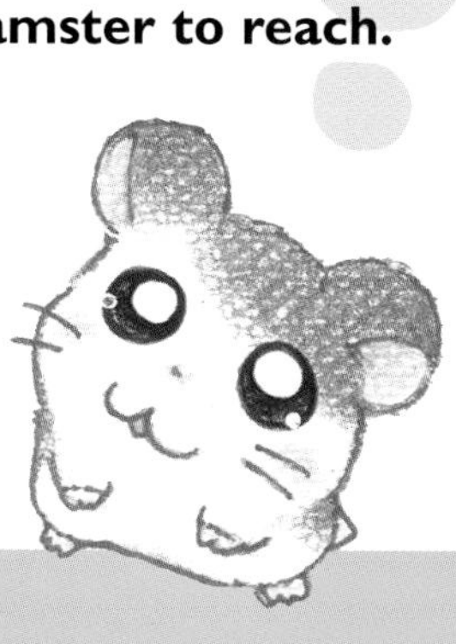

BUYING A HAMSTER HOUSE.

You can buy a cage especially made for hamsters at the pet store.

WIRE CAGE

Choose a cage that has only one level and is low in height.

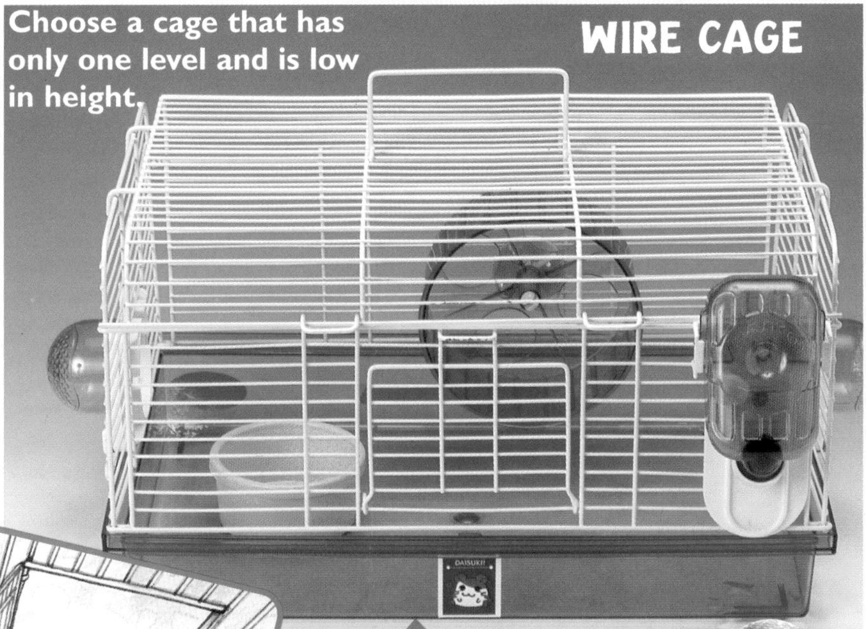

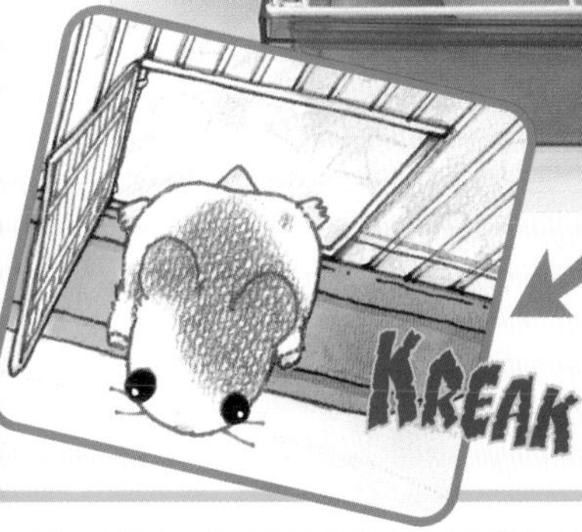
KREAK

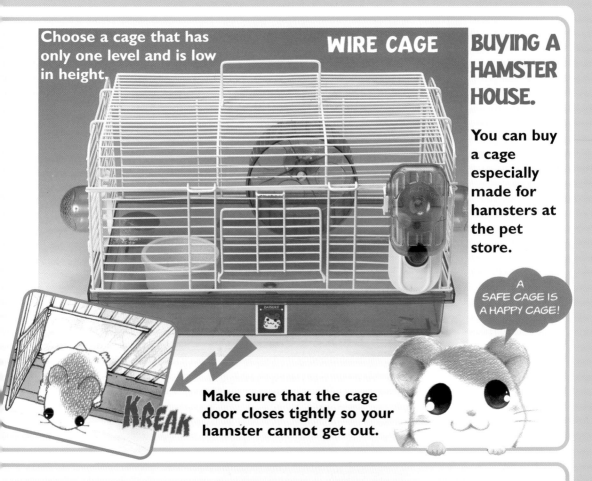

Make sure that the cage door closes tightly so your hamster cannot get out.

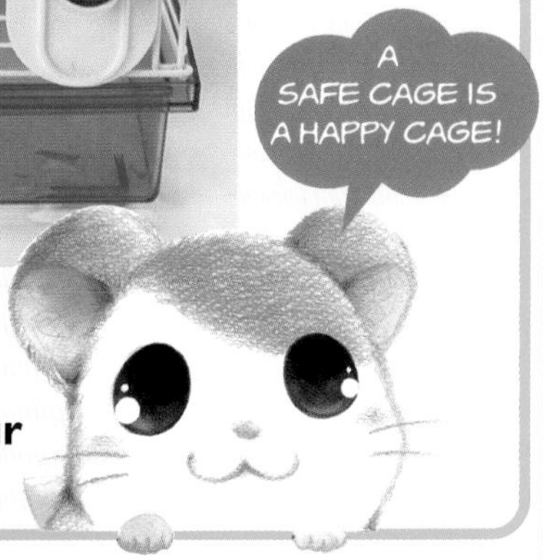
A SAFE CAGE IS A HAPPY CAGE!

PLASTIC CAGE

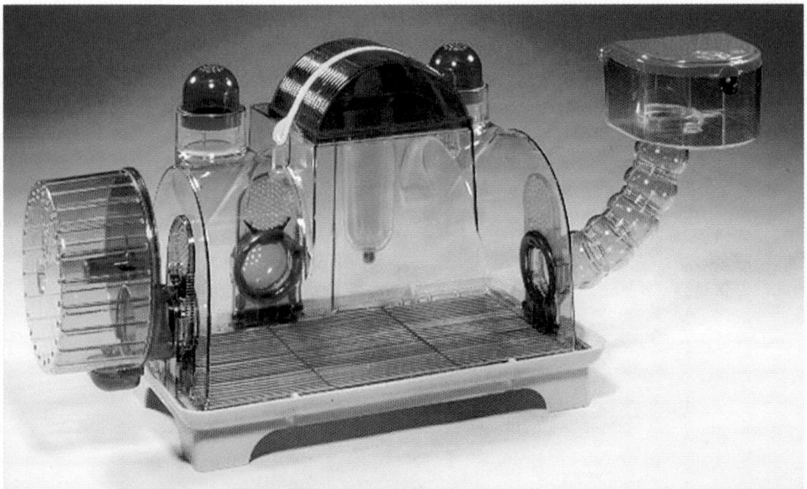

The smooth plastic walls prevent a hamster from climbing too high and hurting itself.

Be careful not to block the ventilation holes!

SETTING UP A HAMSTER CAGE

LIVING QUARTERS AND PLACEMENT

A hamster's living quarters must be both spacious and safe. Hamsters can hurt themselves by climbing up the sides of their cage and falling down, therefore a wire mesh cage should have a low ceiling. A plastic-walled cage is recommended.

The following is a description of a prime location for the cage:

- Not too hot, not too cold
- No extreme ranges in temperature
- Well ventilated
- Draft free
- Natural, bright (but indirect) light during the day; no direct sunlight on the cage
- No dogs or cats nearby
- Easy to see
- On a shelf or other sturdy, high place; placing the cage directly on the floor will subject it to vibrations, and floors may be cold or drafty
- Placed next to a wall; being in the center of a room is unsettling to a hamster

HOW TO CHOOSE AND USE HAMSTER EQUIPMENT

NESTING BOX (HAMSTER HOUSE)

Hamsters tend to hide nesting material and food in their nesting boxes. If the nesting box is too small, there may not be enough sleeping space left and the inside of the house will get dirty more easily. Choose a house that is approximately three times the size of the hamster.

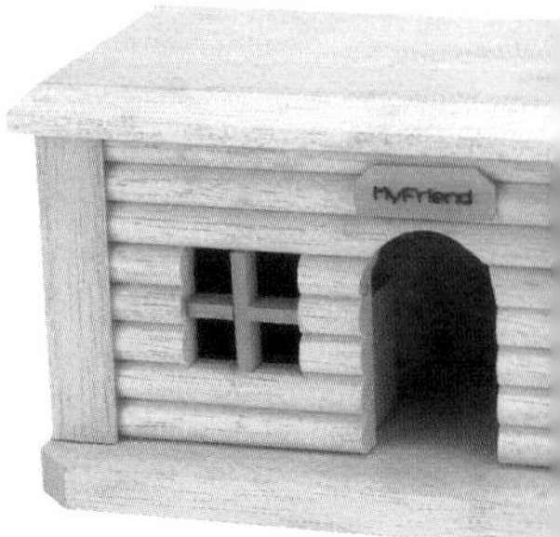
MyFriend

For the nesting box, use wooden one with good ventilation.

FLOOR COVERING, NESTING MATERIAL (BEDDING)

Do not use hay because it damages the hamster's cheek pouches. The best beddings are made from corncob, paper or wood pulp. When using a wire mesh cage, make sure to place a thick layer of bedding to cover the floor in order to prevent injuries from falls. Do not put string, cloth, or tissues in the hamster's home because they can cause injury.

HAMSTER LITTER

To prevent litter from accidentally being ingested or becoming stuck onto any of the feeding dishes, choose the non-clumping type.

HOW TO CHOOSE AND USE HAMSTER TOYS

Place the toys in the cage so that there is free access to play. Choose toys that are safe for your hamster.

Toys for Siberian Hamsters are too small for Golden Hamsters. Select toys suitable for the size of your hamster.

EXERCISE WHEEL

Ladder-type wheels pose a danger of the hamster slipping through the gaps and breaking bones. Choose a wheel without gaps.

PLASTIC TUBES

These tubes can get dirty, so do not construct elaborate set-ups. Sometimes hamsters urinate inside their toys and tubes. Wash all toys frequently.

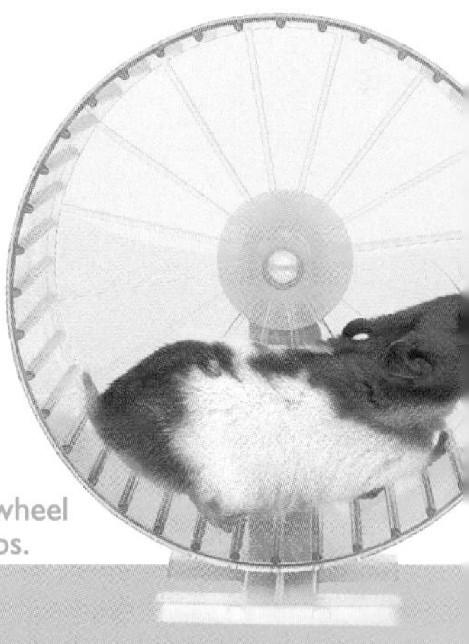

Choose a wheel without gaps.

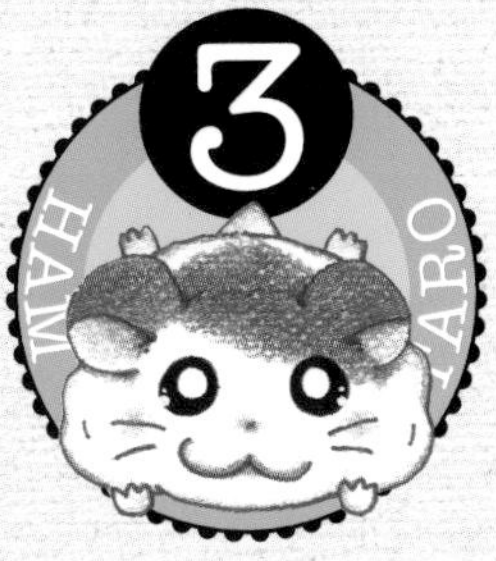
3
HAMTARO

CHAPTER 3 • A HAMSTER'S DAY

HAMSTERS LOVE TO NAP IN THE DAYTIME AND PLAY AT NIGHT.

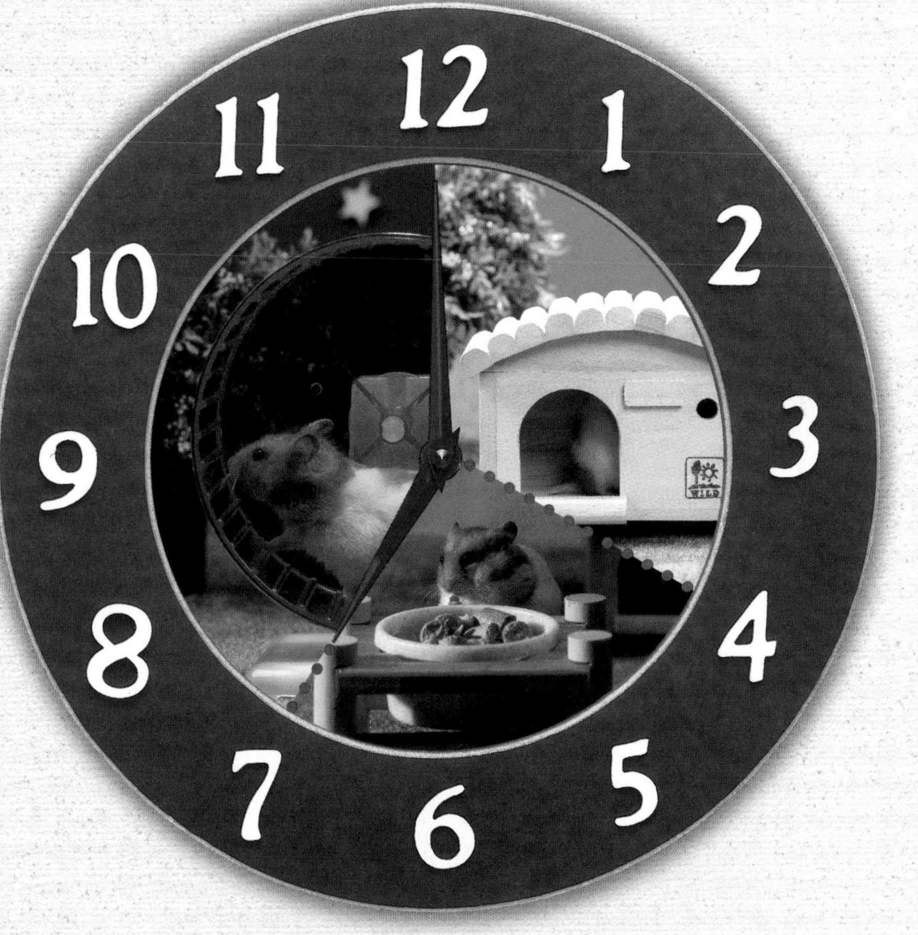
12
1
2
3
4
5
6
7
8
9
10
11

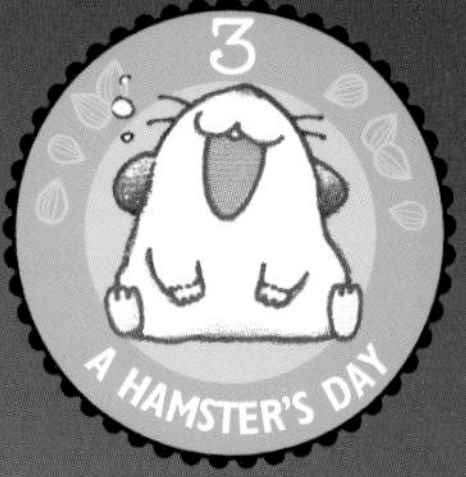
3
A HAMSTER'S DAY

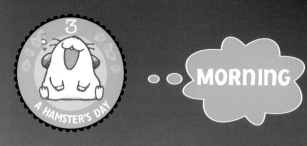

MORNING

DOZING

During the early hours of the morning, hamsters doze in and out of sleep.

Things to do...

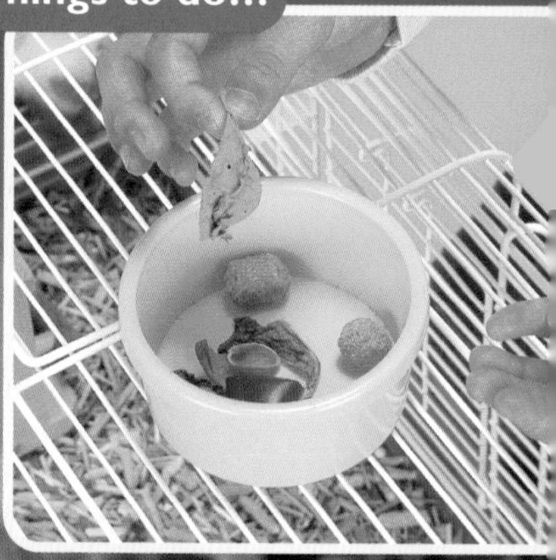

Remove and discard any extra vegetables or fruits that the hamster did not eat, before they spoil. Be sure to do this every day!

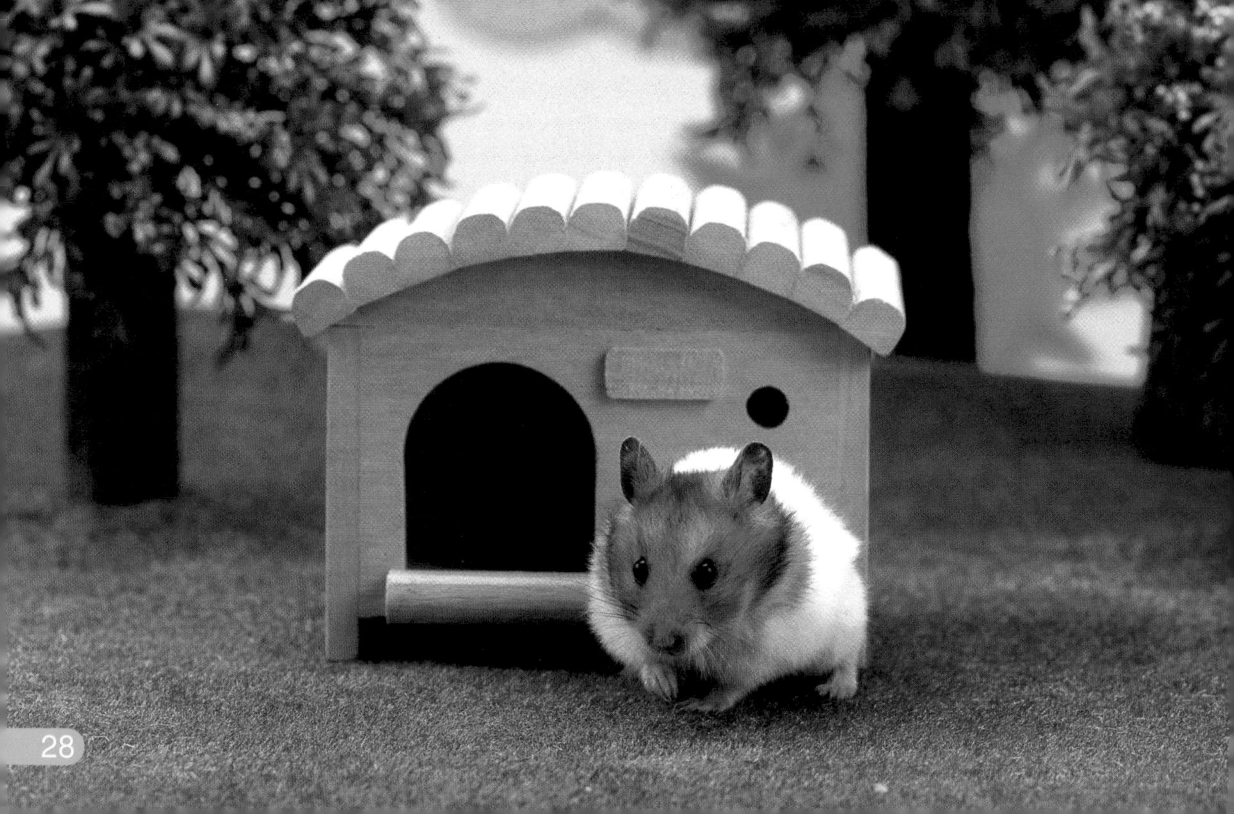

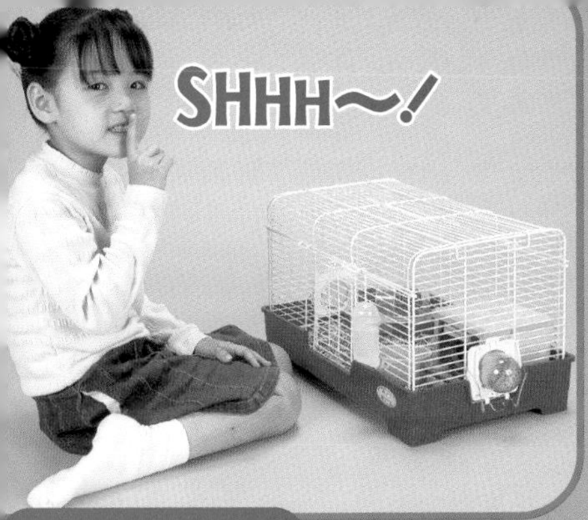
SHHH~!

Things to do...

Keep quiet and let the hamster have a good day's sleep.

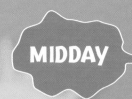

MIDDAY

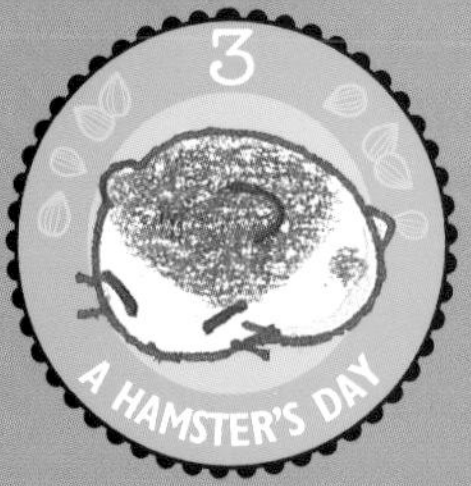
3
A HAMSTER'S DAY

DEEP SLEEP

Midday is the time for the hamster to sleep. It sleeps soundly inside its house.

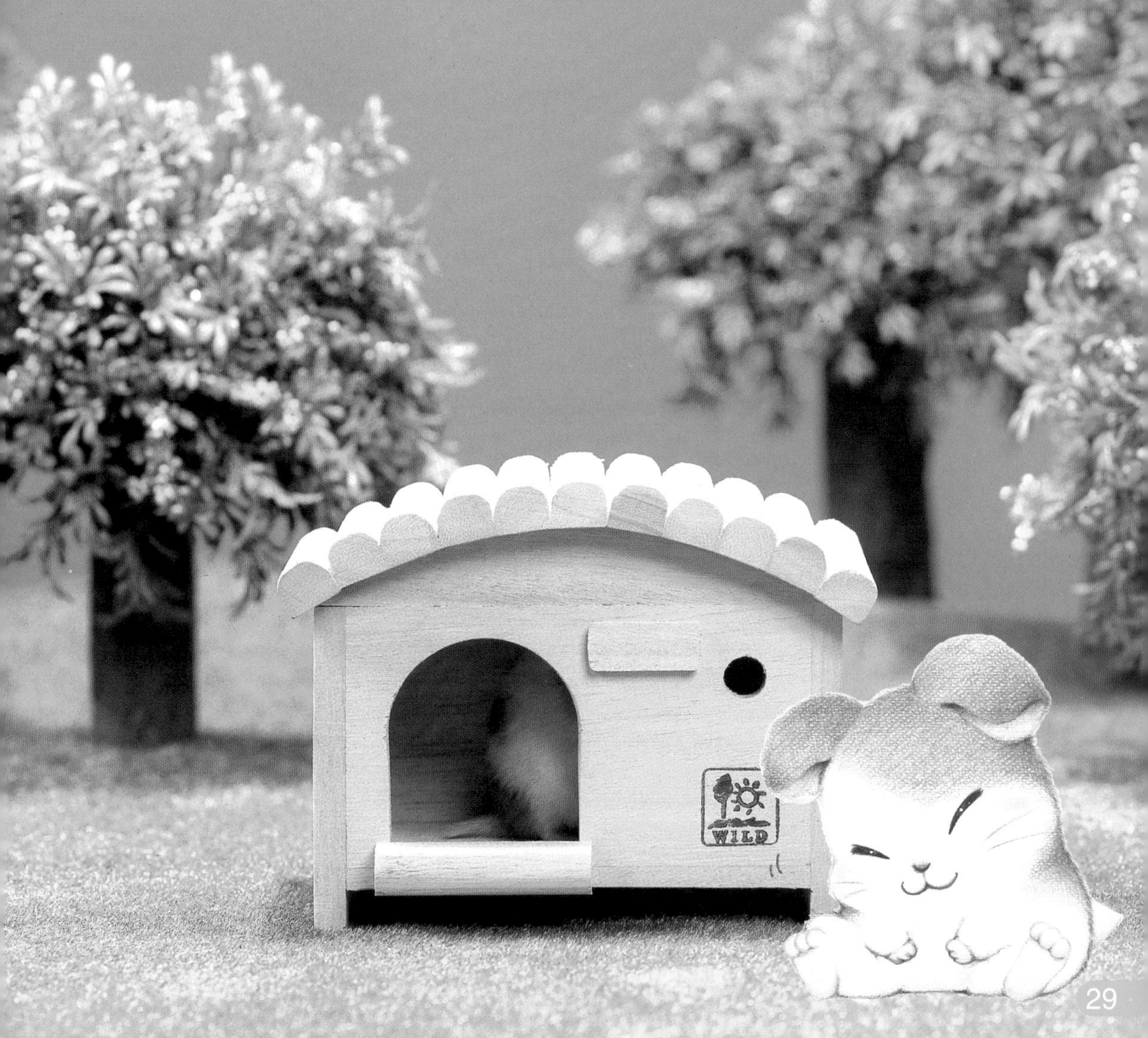
WILD

3
A HAMSTER'S DAY

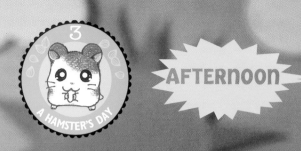

AFTERNOON

HUNGRY!

Hamsters wake up in the late afternoon. They eat a meal, and then start to play. Before its meal, do some housecleaning.

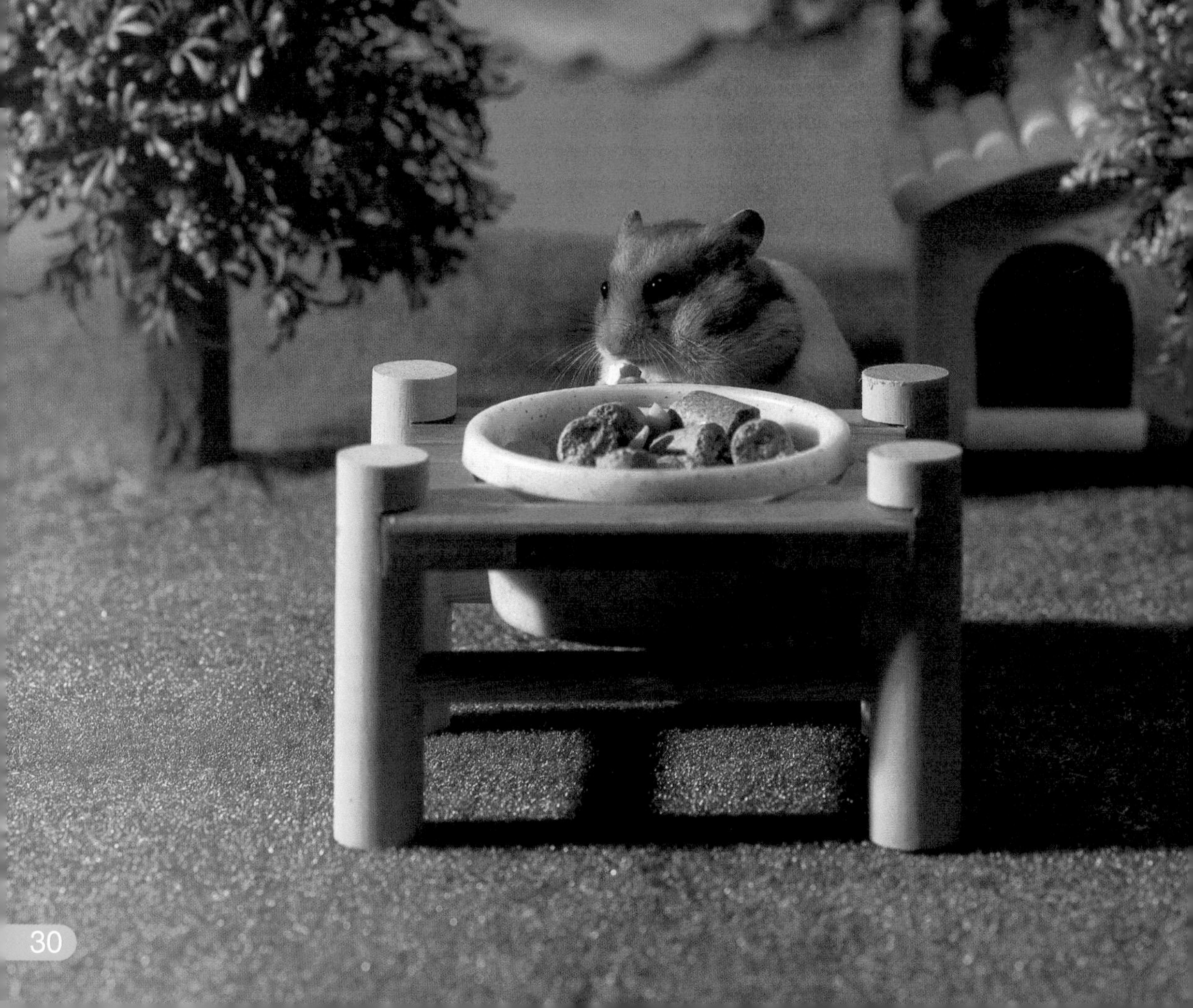

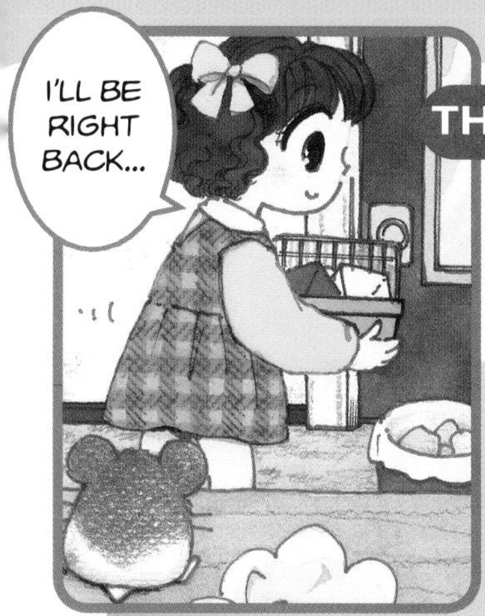
I'LL BE RIGHT BACK...

THINGS TO DO... CLEAN THE HOUSE

Hamsters like to eat and play at a regular time. It's a good thing to have a set time every day to clean their cage, too.

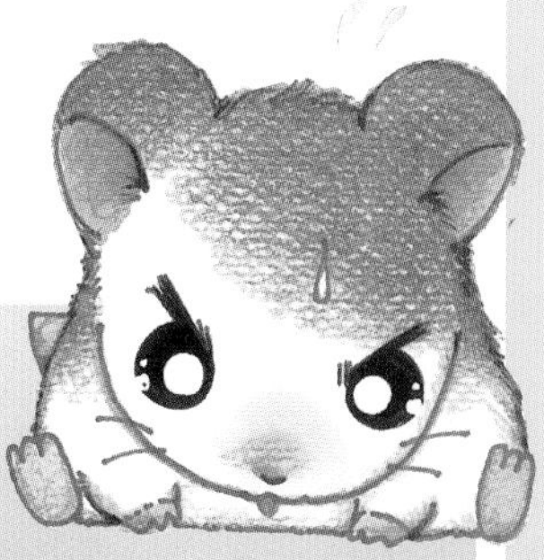

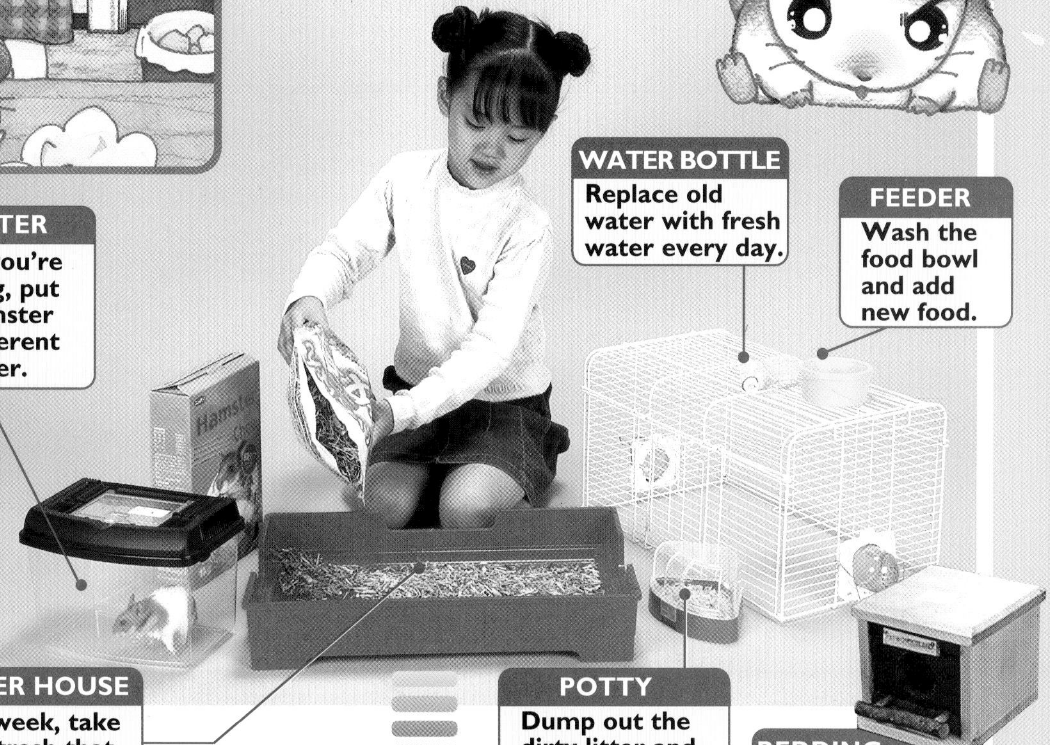

WATER BOTTLE
Replace old water with fresh water every day.

FEEDER
Wash the food bowl and add new food.

HAMSTER
While you're cleaning, put the hamster in a different container.

HAMSTER HOUSE
Once a week, take out any trash that is inside.

POTTY
Dump out the dirty litter and replace it with fresh.

BEDDING
First, scoop out any soiled spots and trash, then add clean bedding. Once a week, replace all the bedding.

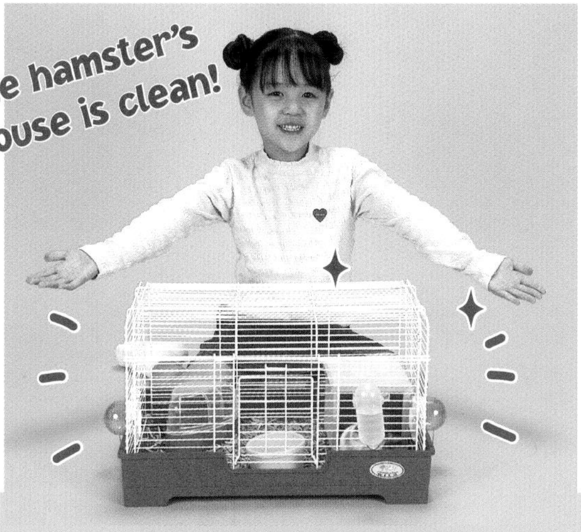
The hamster's house is clean!

Do a major cleaning once a month.
Wash the cage and furniture with water and let dry thoroughly.

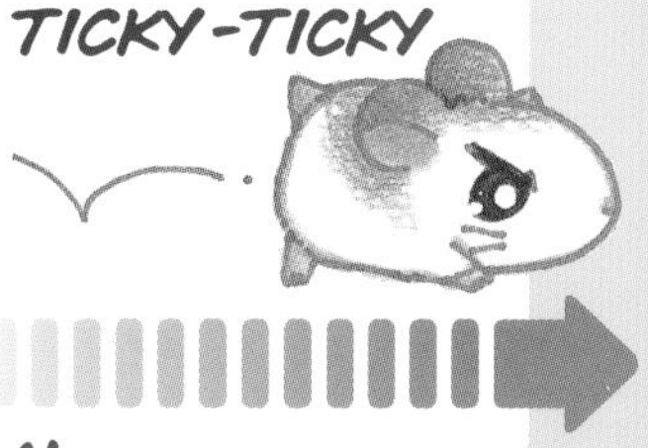
TICKY-TICKY

Now, finally, it's time to eat!

HAM-HA

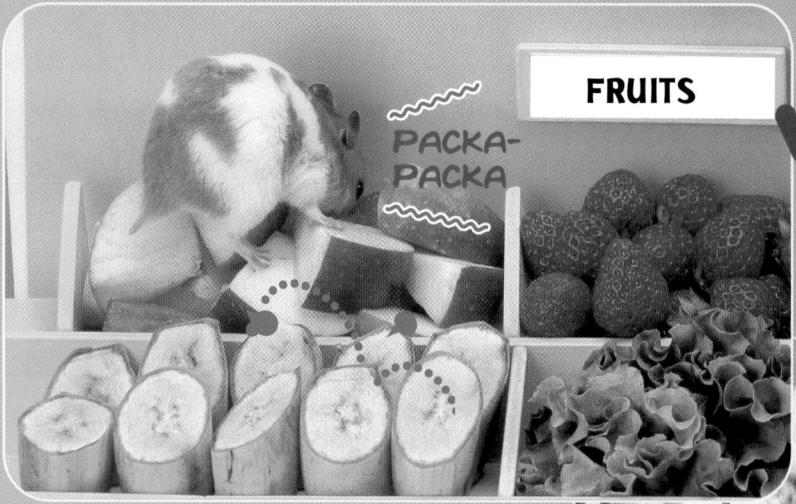
FRUITS
PACKA-
PACKA

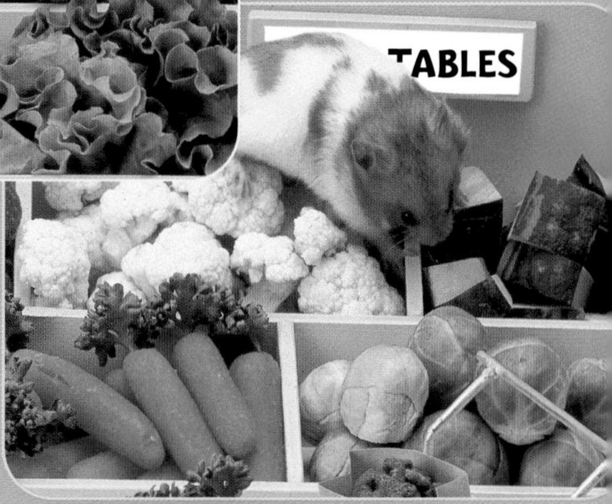
TABLES

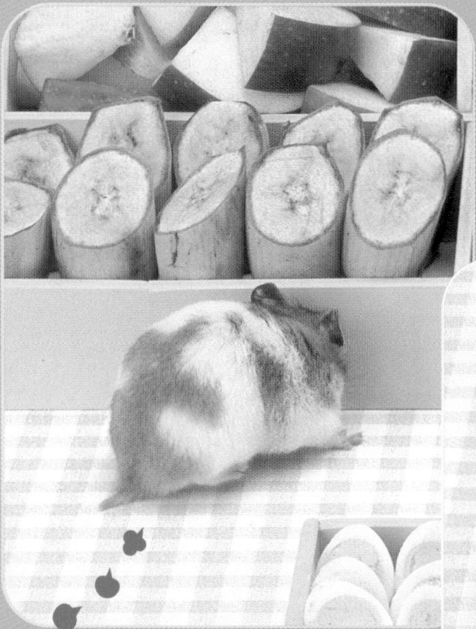

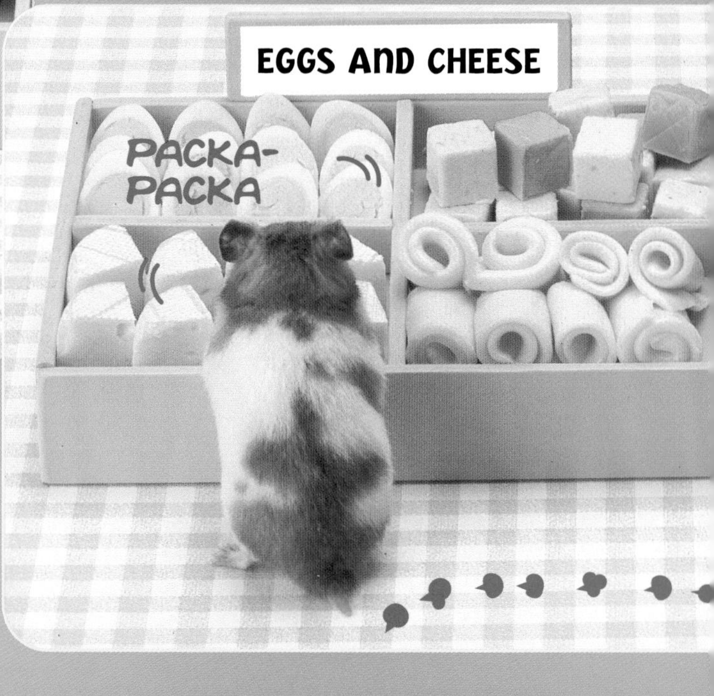
EGGS AND CHEESE
PACKA-
PACKA

UPERMARKET

THINGS TO DO...

PREPARING FOOD FOR YOUR HAMSTER.

After housecleaning, it's time for a tasty meal. Gather a variety of nutritious foods.

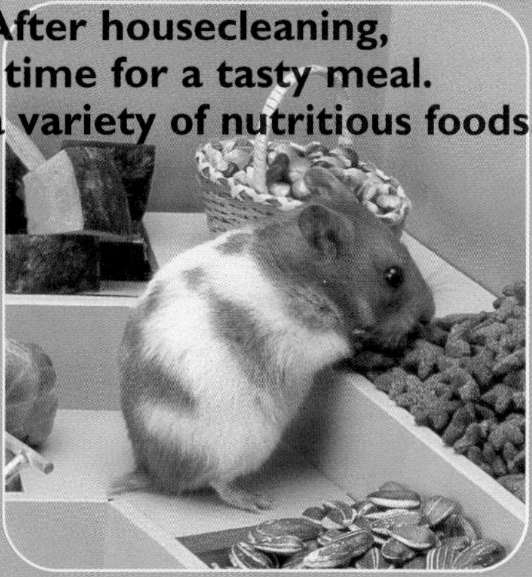

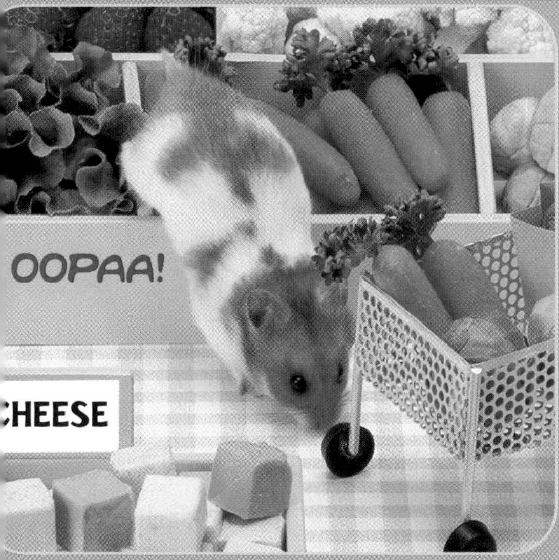
OOPAA!
HEESE

PET CORNER

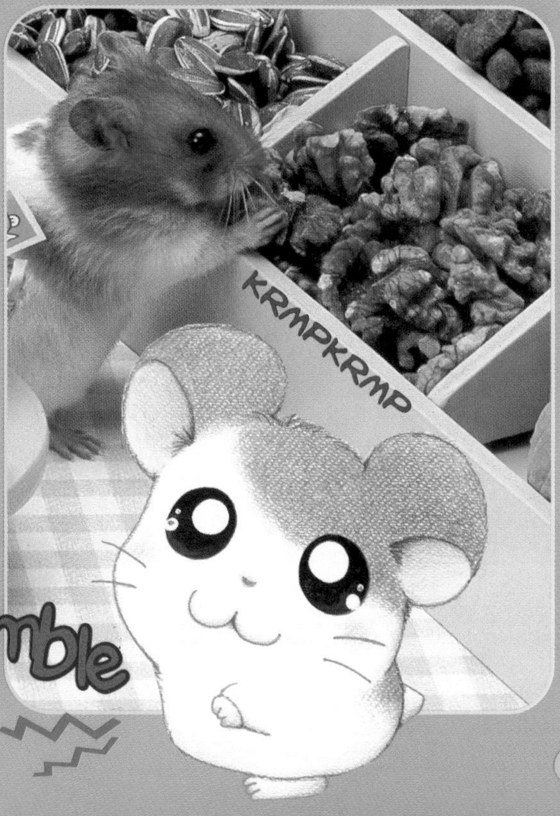
KRMPKRMP
Rumble

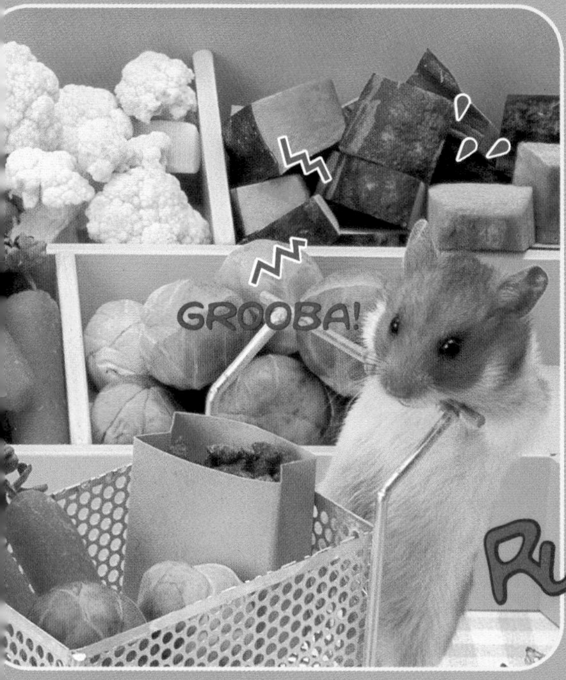
GROOBA!

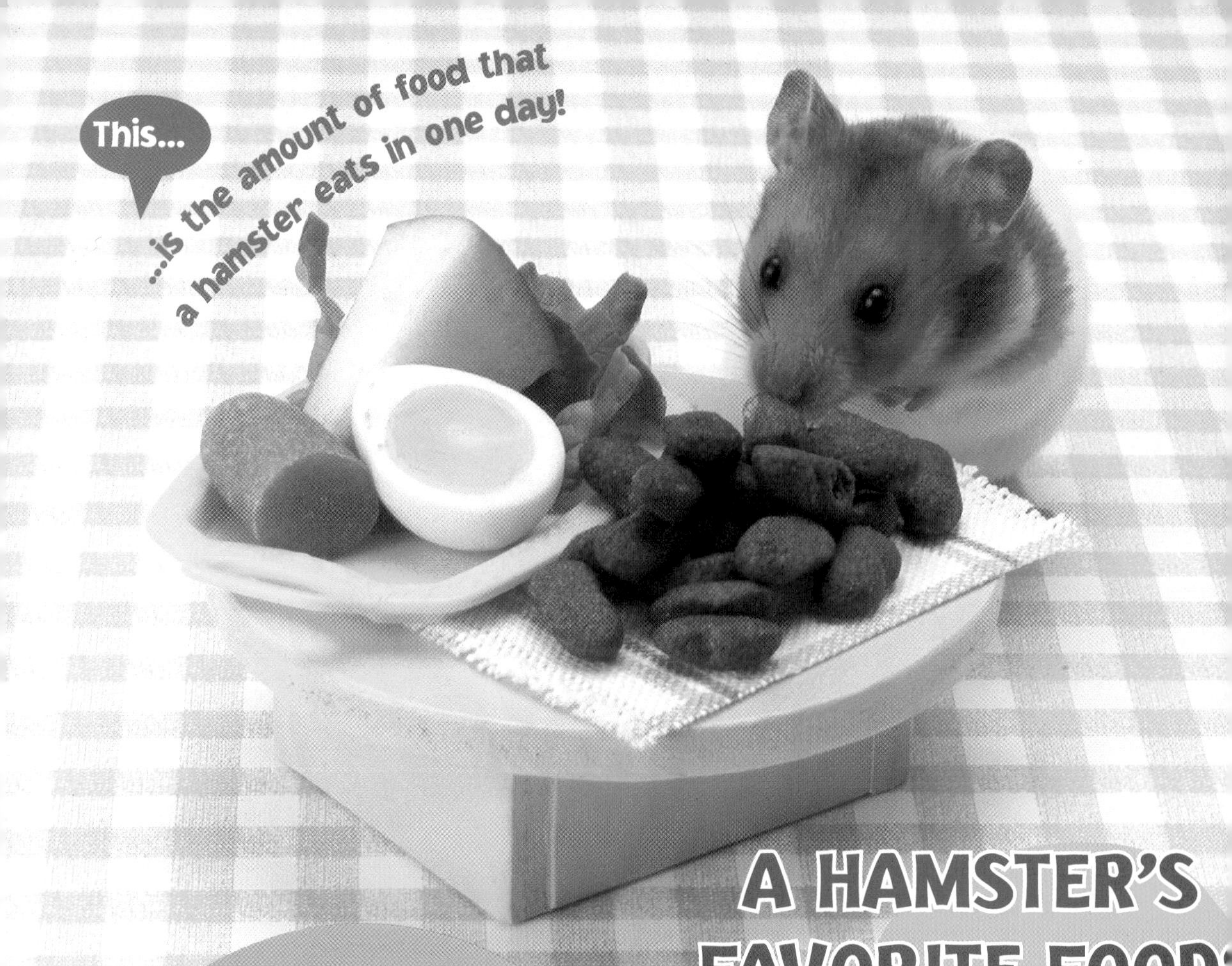
This...
...is the amount of food that a hamster eats in one day!

A HAMSTER'S FAVORITE FOOD

MAIN COURSE

HAMSTER FOOD

Hamster food contains all the nutrition necessary for hamsters and should make up most of what they eat. You can buy it at a pet store.

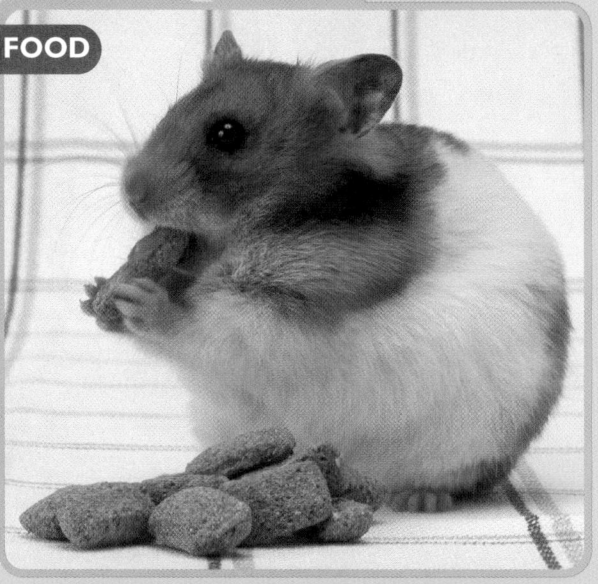

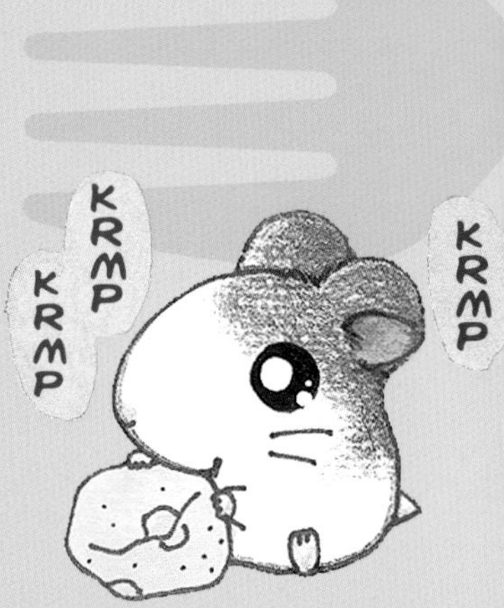
KRMP
KRMP
KRMP

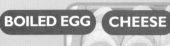

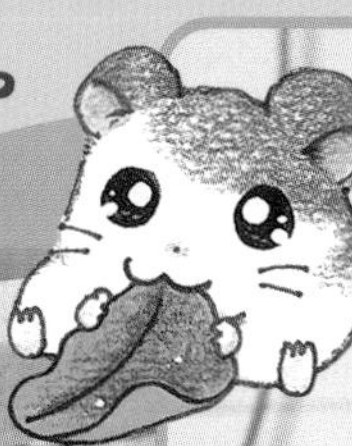
KRMPKRMP

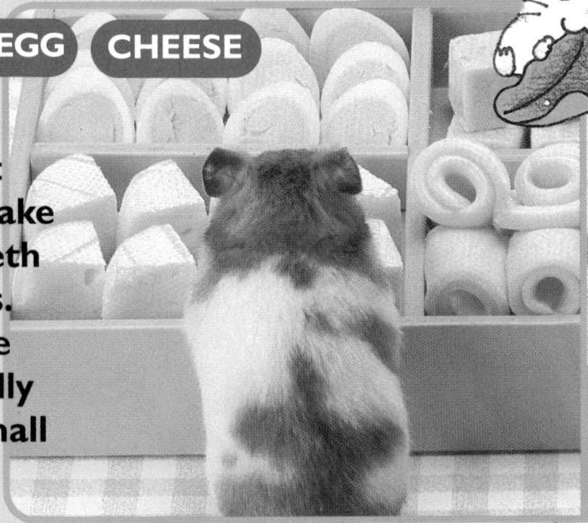
BOILED EGG
CHEESE

These are foods that help to make strong teeth and bones. Give these occasionally in very small amounts.

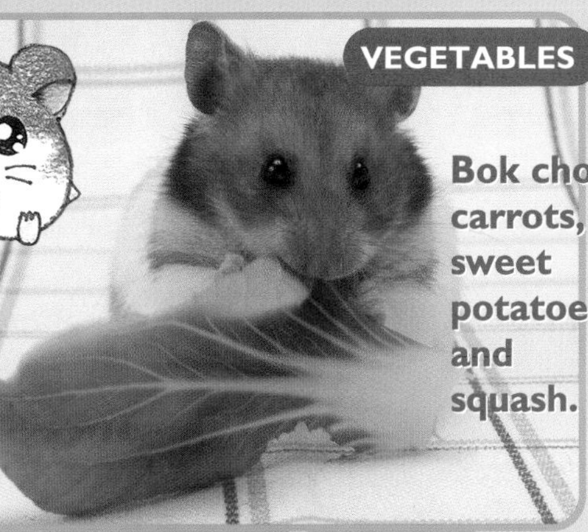
VEGETABLES

Bok choy, carrots, sweet potatoes, and squash.

SIDE DISHES

Fresh vegetables help to make a hamster resistant to illness.

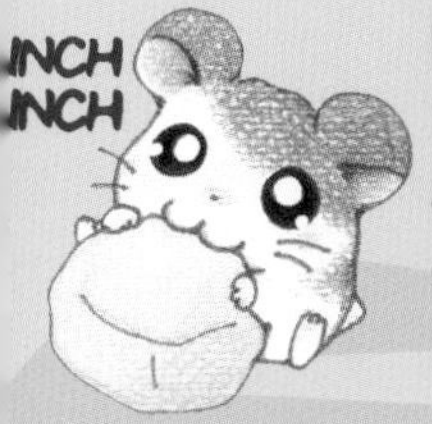
NCH
NCH

Apples, bananas, strawberries and oranges... Don't leave fruit in the cage, because they will spoil and make your hamster sick.

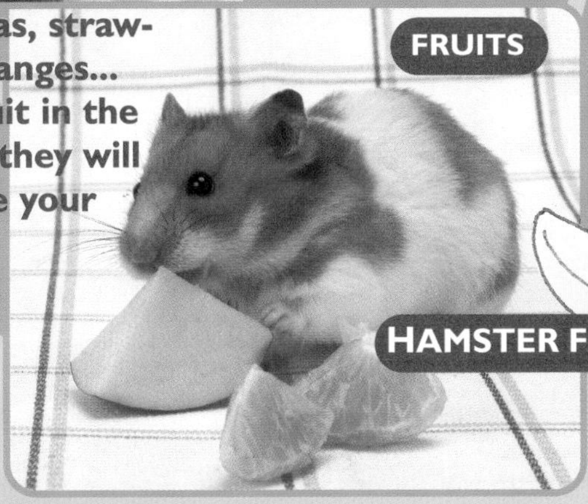
FRUITS

Sweet fruits are a great source of energy.

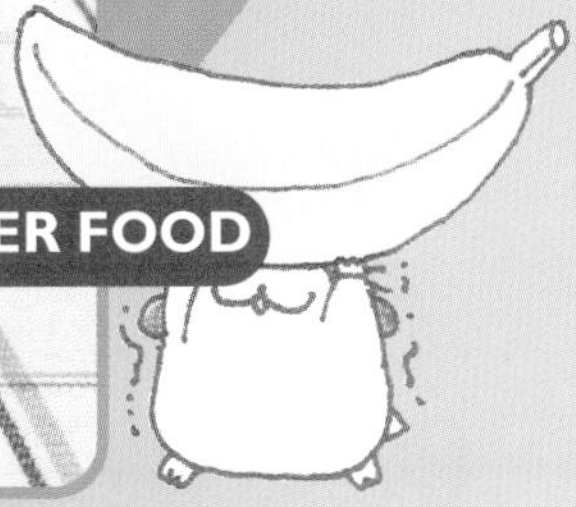
HAMSTER FOOD

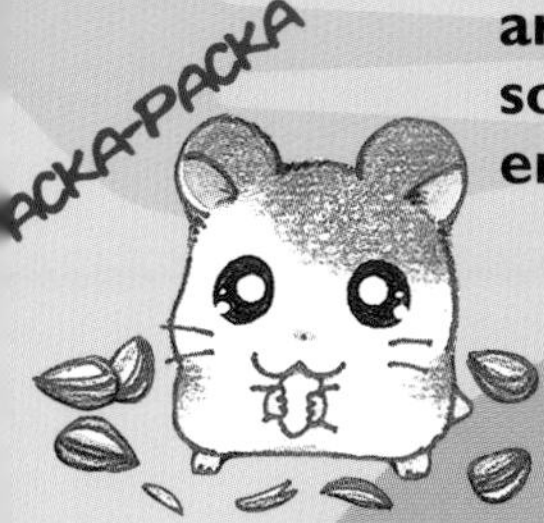
PACKA-PACKA

nuts

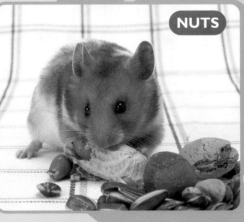

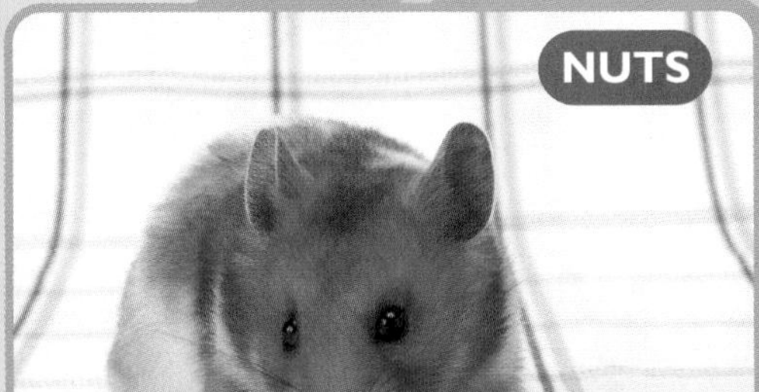
NUTS

Hamsters love nuts and seeds. Since they might eat too many of these treats, give them just a little at the end of their meal.

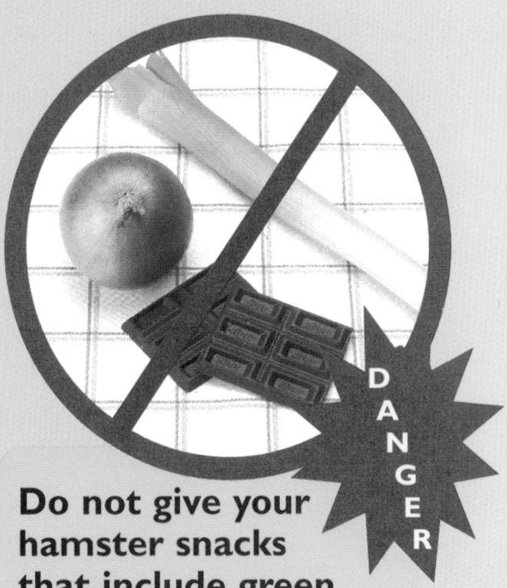
DANGER

Do not give your hamster snacks that include green onions, onions, or chocolate. These can kill your hamster!

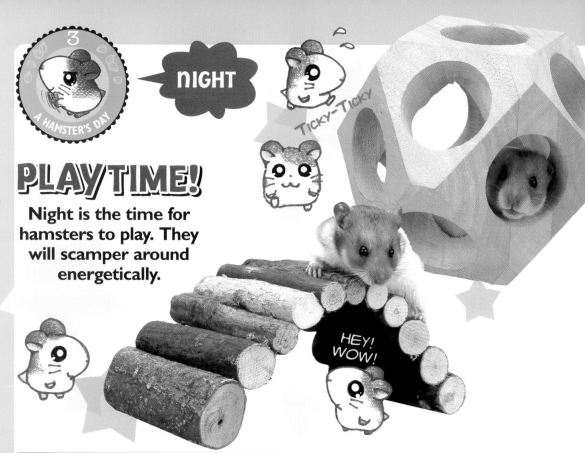

3

A HAMSTER'S DAY

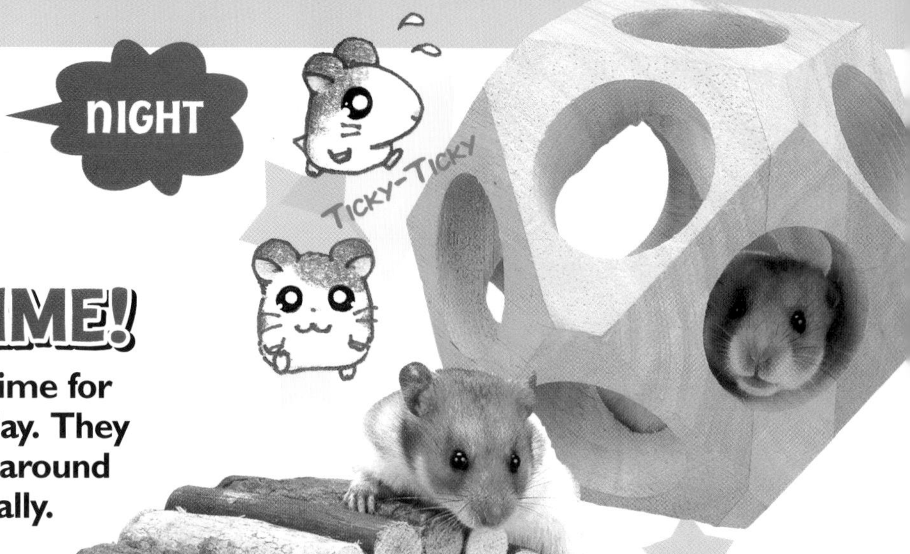
NIGHT
TICKY-TICKY

PLAYTIME!

Night is the time for hamsters to play. They will scamper around energetically.

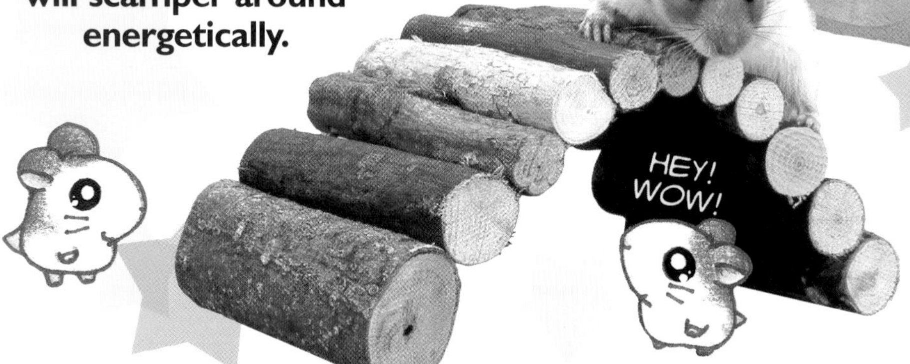
HEY!
WOW!

Play with your hamster!

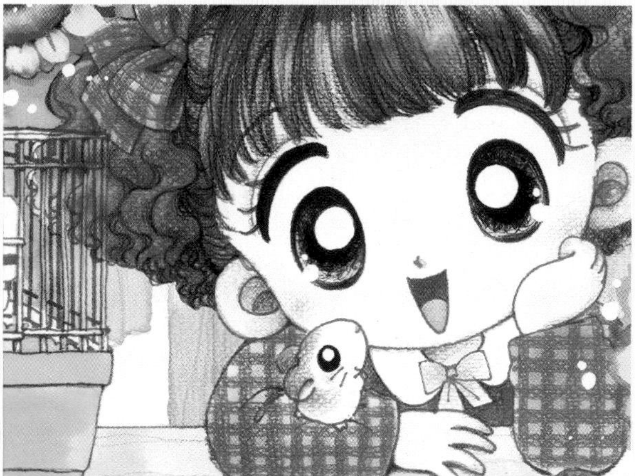

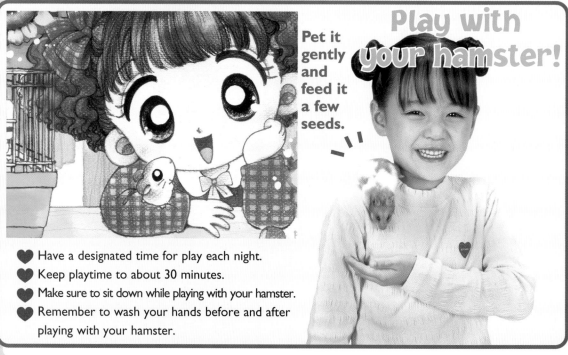

Pet it gently and feed it a few seeds.

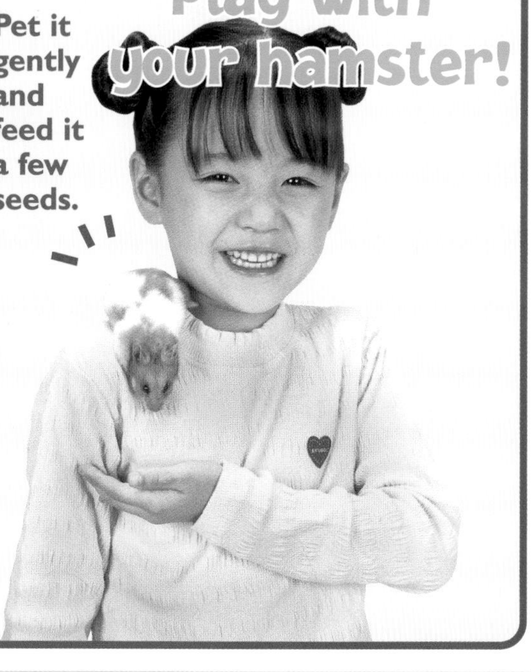

- Have a designated time for play each night.
- Keep playtime to about 30 minutes.
- Make sure to sit down while playing with your hamster.
- Remember to wash your hands before and after playing with your hamster.

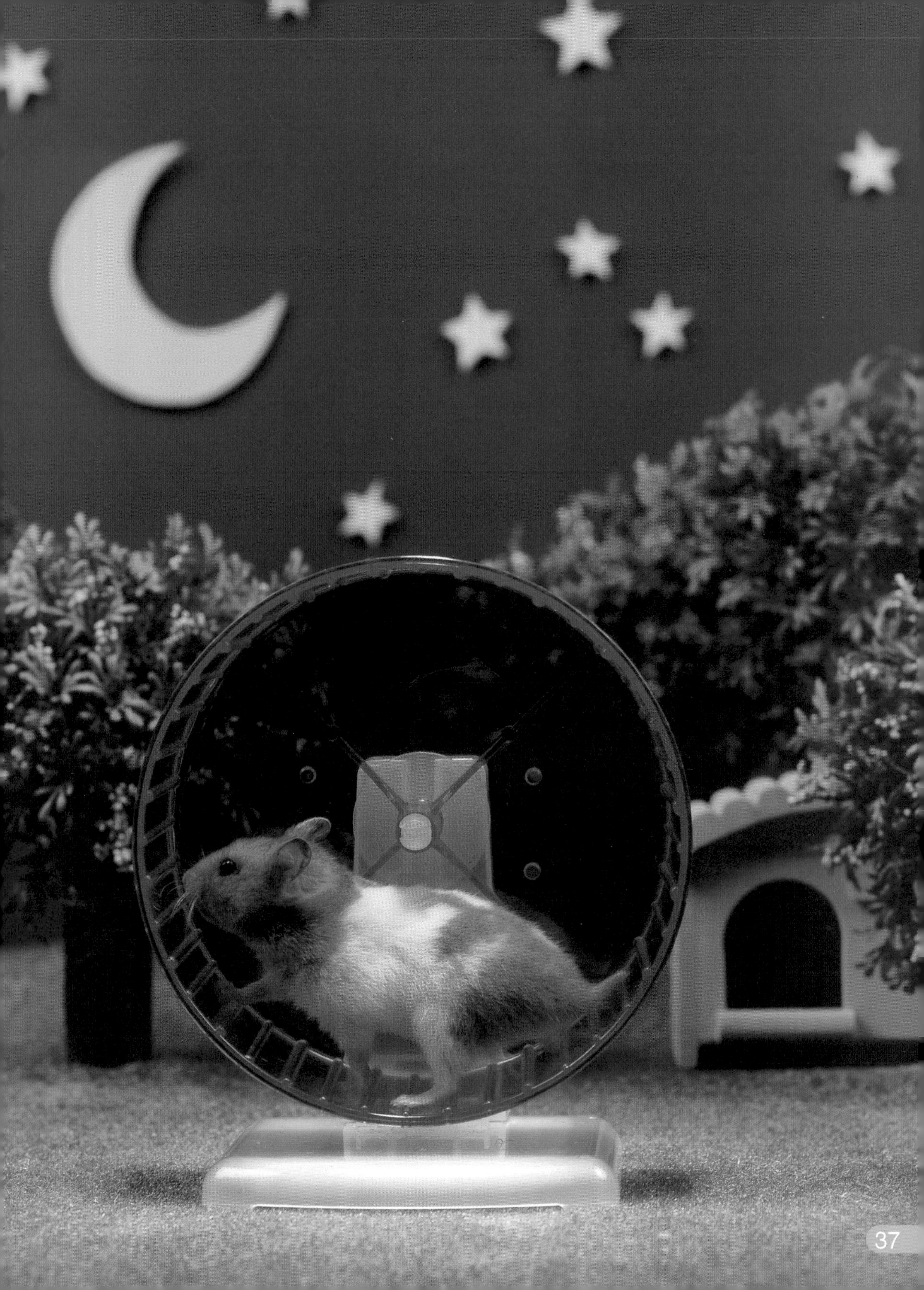

HAM-HAM QUESTIO

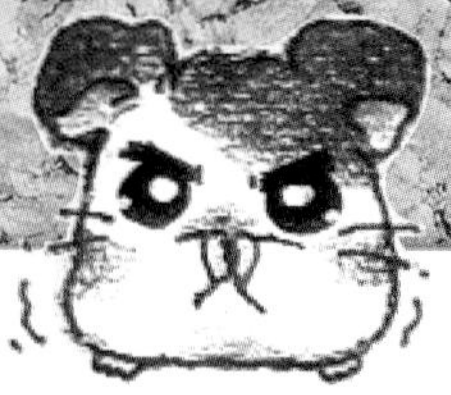

Do hamsters need special care during winter and summer?

Cold weather is very dangerous to us. If it is too cold, we go into continuous hibernation and might even end up dying. So, when it gets cold, please keep the room warm. Also, we really don't like very hot weather either. When it's hot, we get tired. So, during the summer, please keep us in a cool room.

For more details, read page 54.

When my hamster is playing at night, is it better to keep the lights on?

Humans tend to wake up when it becomes light and get sleepy at night, but we hamsters are the exact opposite. We start to wake in the late afternoon when it gets darker, and then eat our meals and play. When morning comes and it gets lighter, we go back to our homes and go to sleep. When we are awake, we like it better dark, so at night, keep the room where the cage is dark.

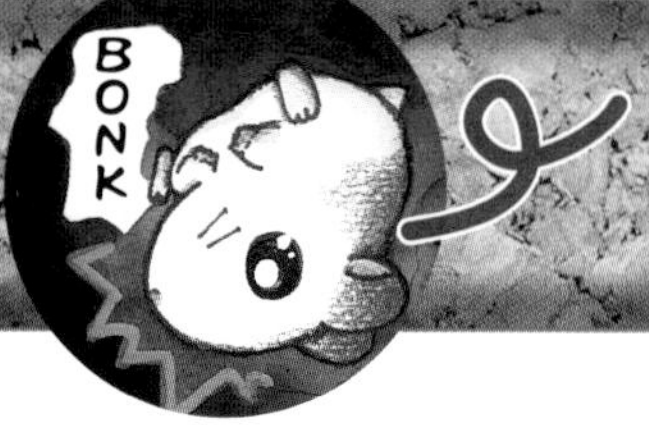
BONK

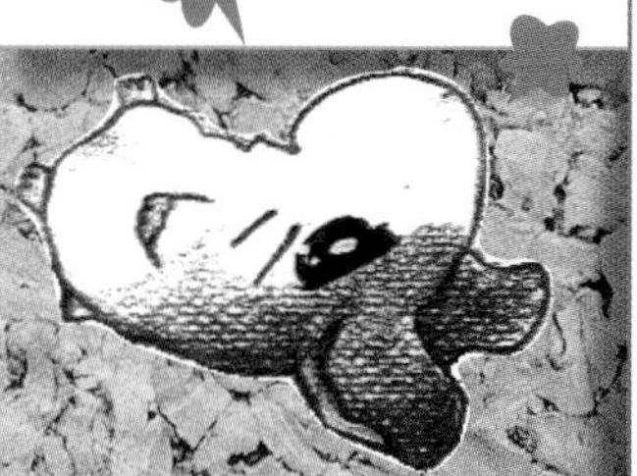

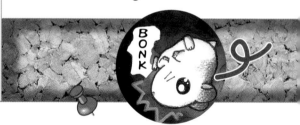

I'm having a hard time making friends with my hamster. What should I do?

Hamsters like people who care for them in a gentle manner, but it still might take some time to become friends with your hamster. Some hamsters are more shy or aggressive than others. In those cases, present your hamster with a few sunflower seeds! It makes us very happy if we're given sunflower seeds every day by hand. Even if we get startled and bite, please don't yell at us in a big voice or hit us–please be kind and patient.

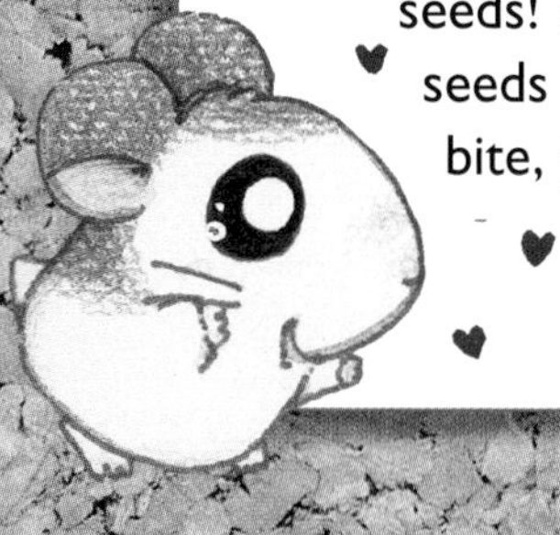

ULLETIN BOARD

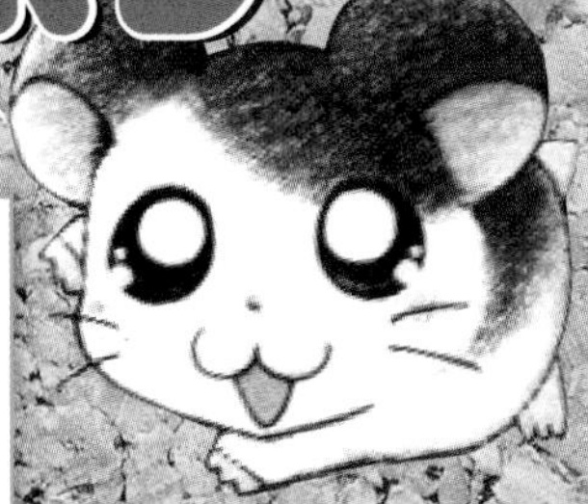

Aren't hamsters lonely being all by themselves?

Wild hamsters usually live alone. When they are small, they live with their mother, but adult hamsters like to live by themselves. They're not lonely at all, in fact, hamsters will fight if they are placed together. So be sure to keep each hamster in its own cage.

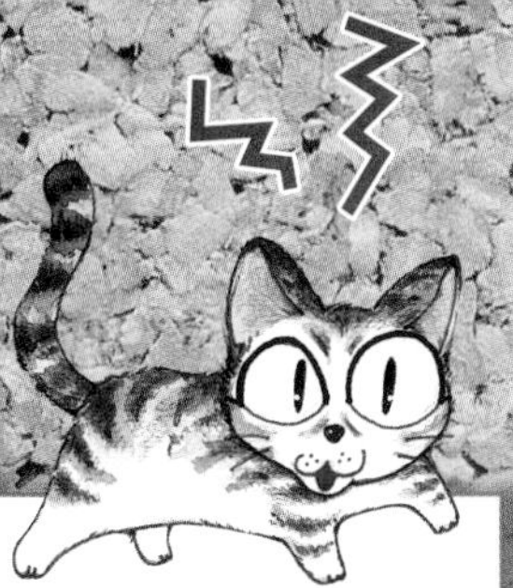

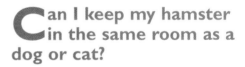

Can I keep my hamster in the same room as a dog or cat?

Hamsters definitely don't like that! Dogs and cats are known to be mean to us and even kill us! Because hamsters are so much smaller than dogs and cats, we would never be able to win in a fight. Even the smell of them scares us, so please don't bring dogs or cats nearby.

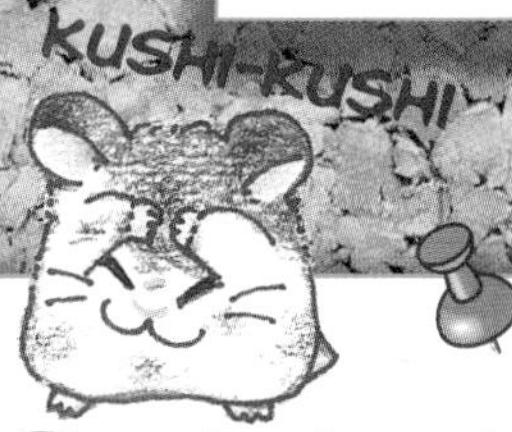
KUSHI-KUSHI

Can I take a bath with my hamster?

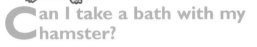

That would be dangerous, because we can't swim! And having hot or cold water splashed on our bodies shocks us, and might make us sick. So please don't put us in the bathtub or scrub us with soap. We groom ourselves so we don't need to take a bath.

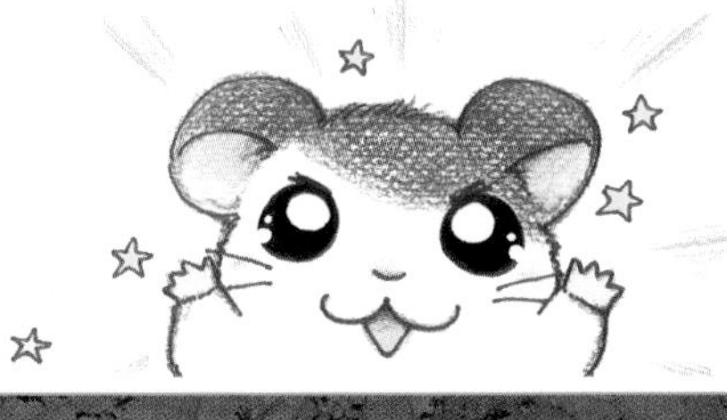

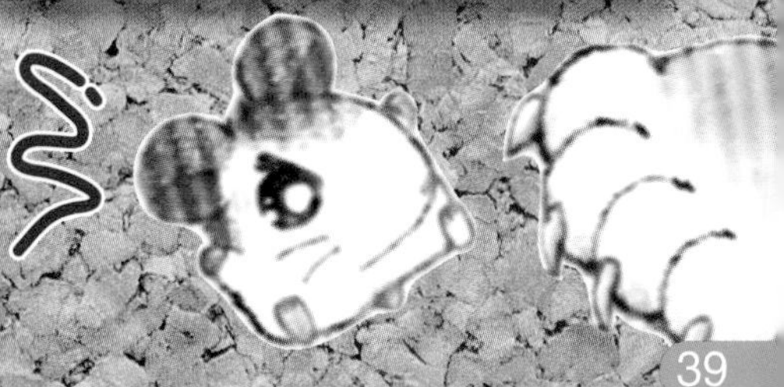

TIPS ON HAMSTER CARE

 HOW TO CHOOSE YOUR HAMSTER'S FOOD.

In order to keep your hamster healthy, a nutritionally balanced diet is very important.

STAPLE FOODS

The main diet should consist of hamster food (a dry solid meal made especially for hamsters, often in the form of pellets). Choose the kind that does not contain various types of sunflower seeds. Because hamsters love sunflower seeds more than the pellets, they might end up eating just the seeds and not the other foods that they need.

FRUITS AND VEGETABLES

First, wash fruits and vegetables thoroughly and dice them into easy-to-handle 1/2-inch cubes before giving them to your hamster.

CHEESE AND BOILED EGGS

These are examples of snacks given to replenish essential animal proteins. Choose cheeses that are low in salt. Give these only as occasional snacks.

NUTS AND OTHER FOODS

Please be careful not to feed your hamster too many nuts or seeds for dessert, because these foods will make your hamster fat and spoil its appetite for other important foods.

FOODS TO AVOID

Do not feed hamsters green onions, onions, potato eyes, sweet desserts or foods with flavoring and seasoning for humans. Foods that are too hot or cold should never be given to hamsters. Cow's milk can cause stomach upset. It is not necessary to add flavoring to your hamster's food.

The amount of food given should be about 5 to 10% of the hamster's body weight. Use hamster pellets as a primary source of food.

 HOW TO CLEAN UP AFTER YOUR HAMSTER

A dirty cage can lead to a sick hamster and can also make the entire room smell bad. Clean your hamster's potty every day, and wash anything it may have urinated on. Some hamsters hoard fruits and vegetables in their nests, so you'll need to inspect their rooms daily and throw out any leftover food.

Hamsters become uncomfortable if their environment does not smell like themselves, so it is not necessary to fully clean out the entire cage every day.

 HOW TO TEACH YOUR HAMSTER TO USE THE POTTY

Hamsters choose their own potty location and use that to urinate. By placing the potty in that location and scattering some urine-soaked bedding on top of the litter, the hamster will gradually learn to use the potty. Some hamsters will not have a set location to urinate. In that case, take care to clean up all the scattered waste. As long as there is daily cleaning of the spots with urine, there should not be residual odor.

Most hamsters do not have a set location for their feces. They cannot be taught to do this in the potty, so please clean up after them during the daily cage cleaning.

RECOMMENDED AMOUNT OF FOOD FOR ONE DAY

(Example for a Golden Hamster weighing 5.3 oz)
Hamster Food… .35 oz (10 gm)
Bok Choy…2 leaves
Carrots…2 cubes
Apple…1 slice
Sunflower Seeds…3 seeds

This is just one example of a recommended daily menu. Various substitutions can be made, for example using sweet potatoes in place of carrots. Limit the intake of animal proteins to once a week.

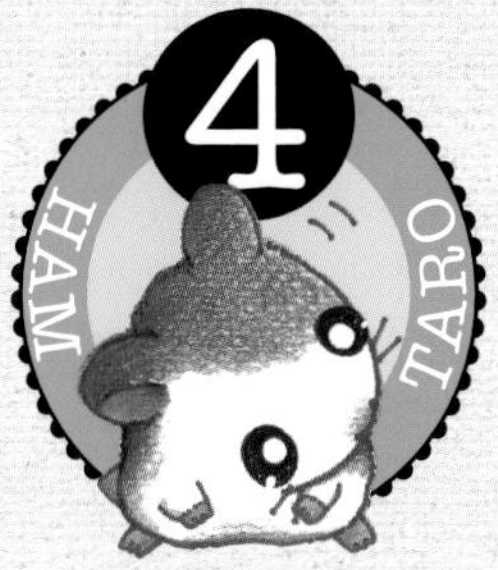
4
HAM
TARO

CHAPTER 4 • HAMSTER PSYCHOLOGY

HAMSTERS LET YOU KNOW HOW THEY FEEL THROUGH BODY LANGUAGE. WATCH AND STUDY YOUR HAMSTER CLOSELY TO UNDERSTAND ITS MOODS.

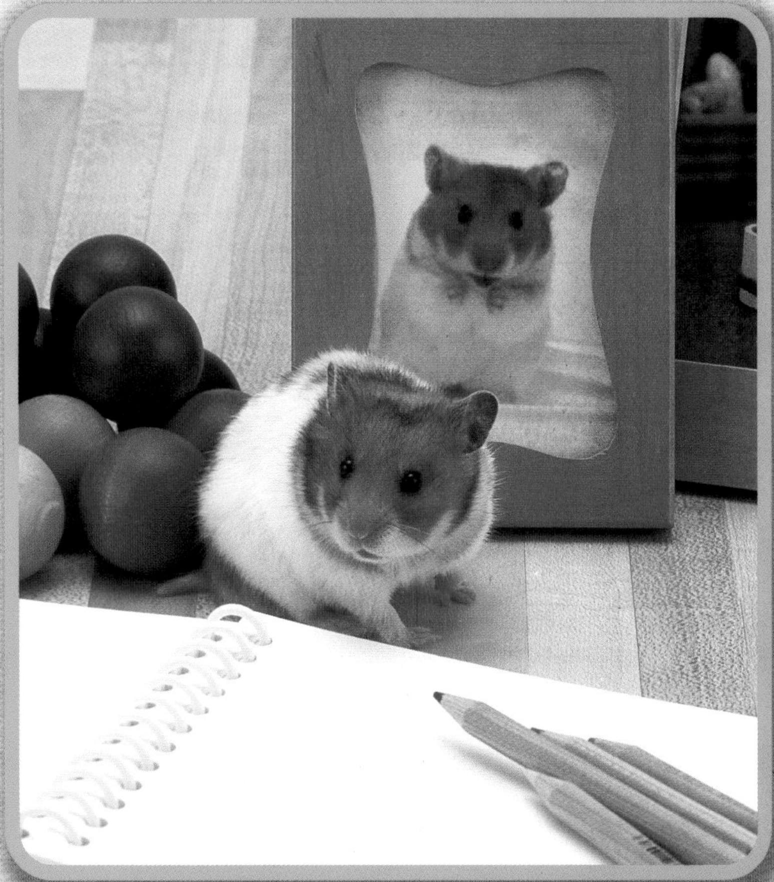

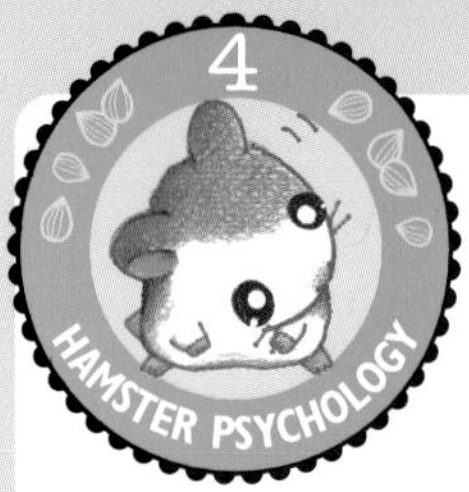
4
HAMSTER PSYCHOLOGY

IF YOU WATCH CAREFULLY, YOU CAN UNDERSTAND

A MESSAGE FROM A HAMSTER

By studying a hamster's body language carefully, you can figure out its mood.

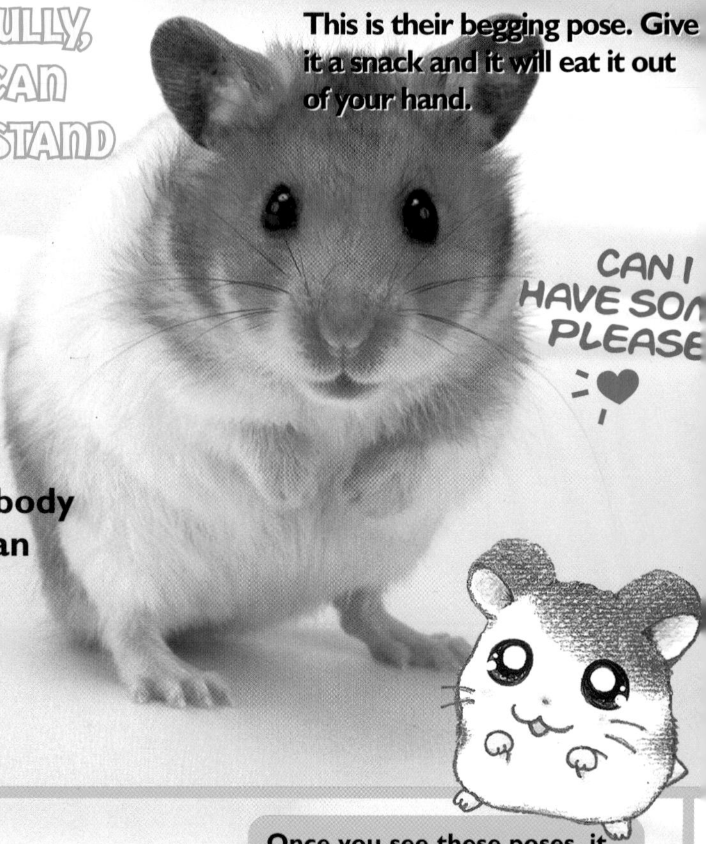
CAN I
HAVE SON
PLEASE

It stands on its hind feet.

This is their begging pose. Give it a snack and it will eat it out of your hand.

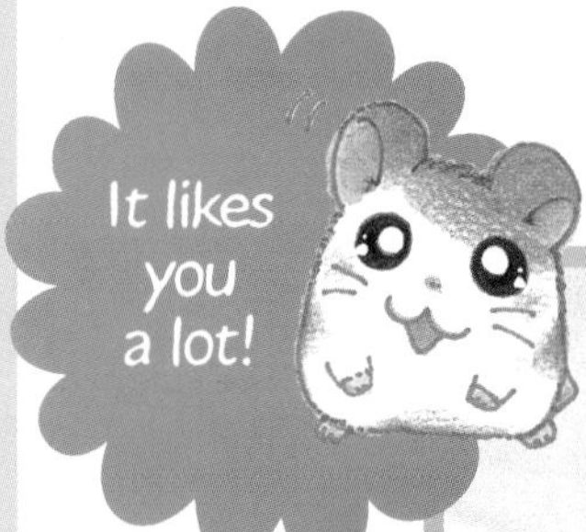
It likes you a lot!

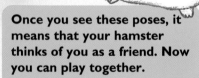

Once you see these poses, it means that your hamster thinks of you as a friend. Now you can play together.

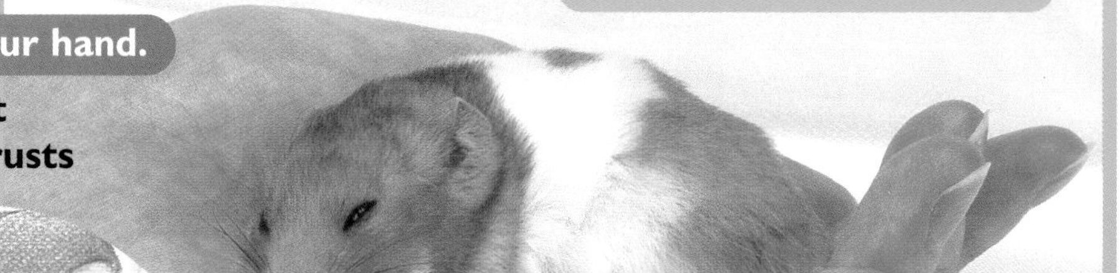
ZUZUZU

It sleeps on your hand.

This means that your hamster trusts you completely. Hold it gently.

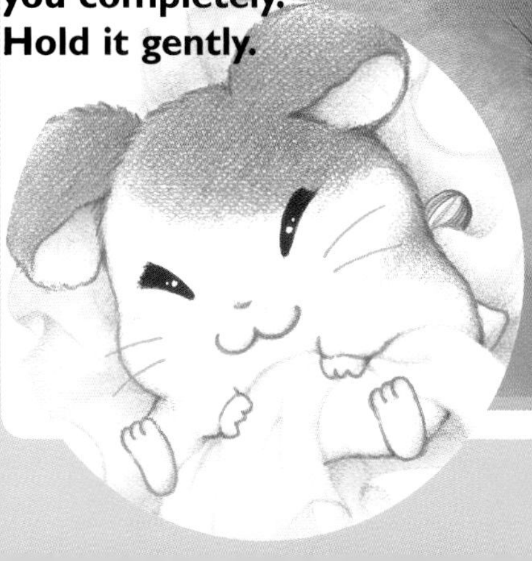

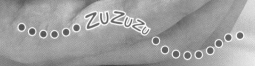

It tries to dig a hole.

Digging a hole in the ground with its hands and mouth makes it feel calm.

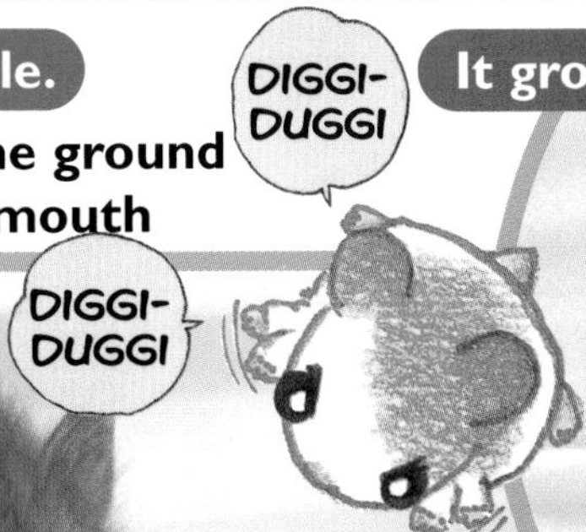
DIGGI-DUGGI
DIGGI-DUGGI

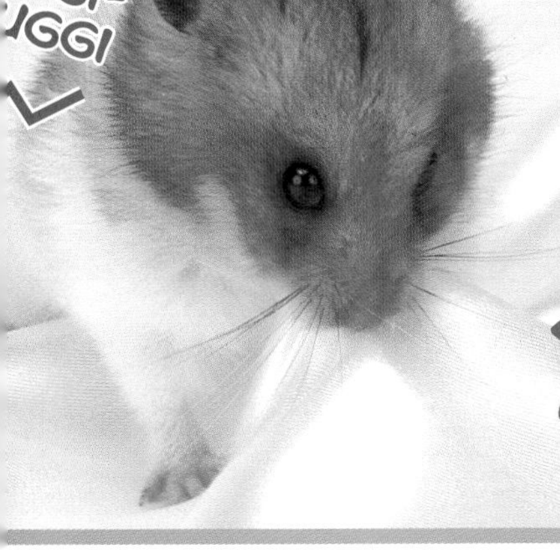

It grooms itself.

When it is nervous, a hamster grooms itself in order to calm down.

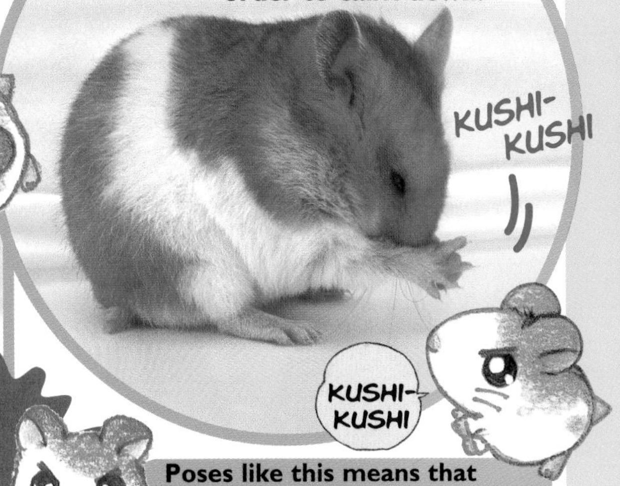
KUSHI-KUSHI
KUSHI-KUSHI

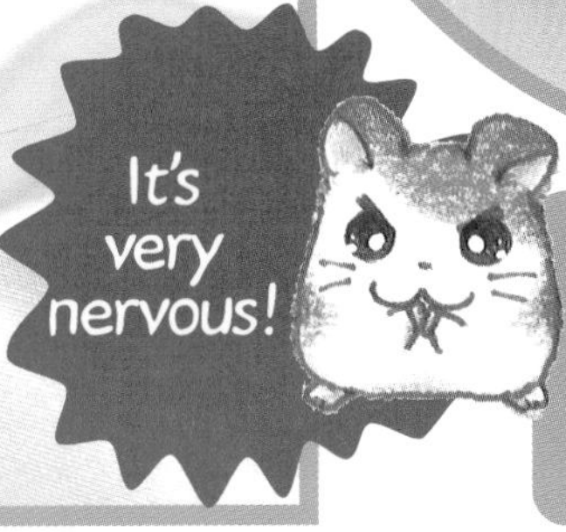
It's very nervous!

Poses like this means that your hamster is not used to you yet and is slightly nervous. When you see this kind of body language, leave it alone until it feels calm again.

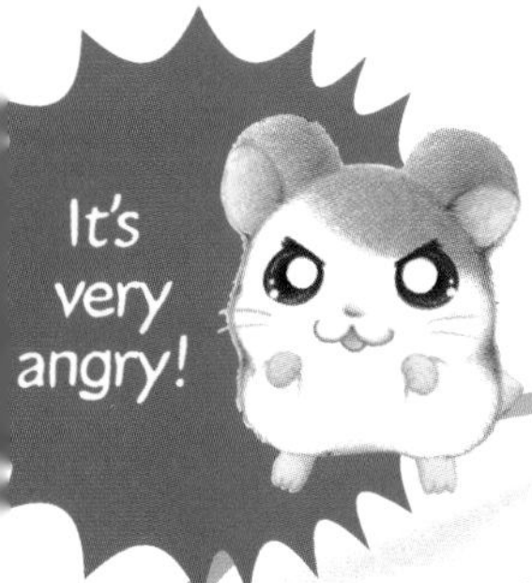
It's very angry!

Your hamster will act like this when it is surprised or angry. Don't handle your hamster then because it might bite.

It raises one paw.

Whenever it is surprised by something—like a loud noise—it will shrink in its neck and raise one paw.

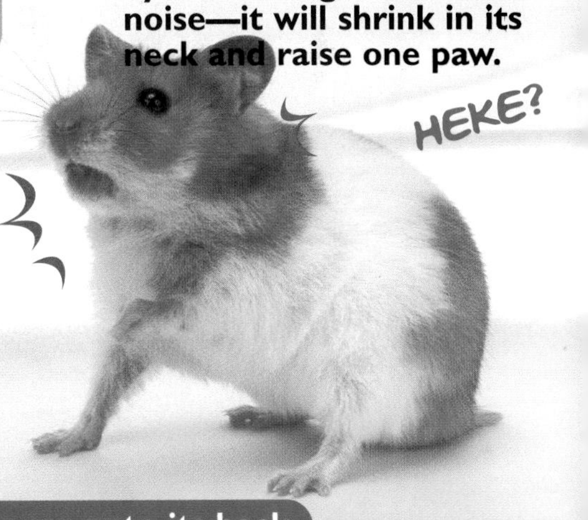
HEKE?

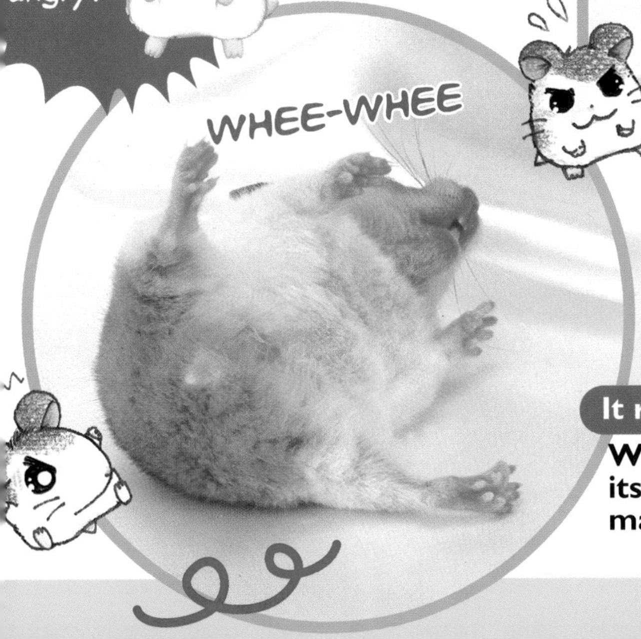
WHEE-WHEE

It rolls over onto its back.

When it is very angry, it will roll onto its back and cry, "Whee-whee!" Don't make your hamster feel like this!

TO MAKE FRIENDS WITH YOUR HAMSTER...

THE GREAT GET-THE-HAMSTER-TO-BE-YOUR-FRIEND ADVENTURE

HAMSTERS LIKE GENTLE AND NICE FRIENDS. DO ALL FOUR STEPS TO BECOME YOUR HAMSTER'S BEST FRIEND.

STEP 1

GIVE YOUR HAMSTER A NAME AND CALL IT BY THAT NAME.

Talk to your hamster and call it by its name when it is awake. When your hamster gets used to this, it will begin to look when its name is called.

CHECKPOINTS

Happy It wants its name to be called out softly.

Unhappy It is scared when its name is yelled out in a loud voice.

STEP 2

GIVE IT A SNACK.

Hamsters love snacks like nuts and sunflower seeds. Try to hand feed a little bit to your hamster.

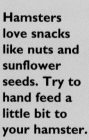

CHECKPOINTS

Happy It would like a snack at a set time every day.

Unhappy Too many snacks will cause it to get fat.

KRMP-KRMP

KRMP-KRMP

PROMISE #1

I will only play with my hamster when it is awake.

ROMISE #2

will not frighten ny hamster.

PROMISE #3

I will wash my hands before and after playing with my hamster.

STROKE IT GENTLY. STEP 3

When your hamster gets more used to you, try stroking it gently. Stroke it after you call it by its name.

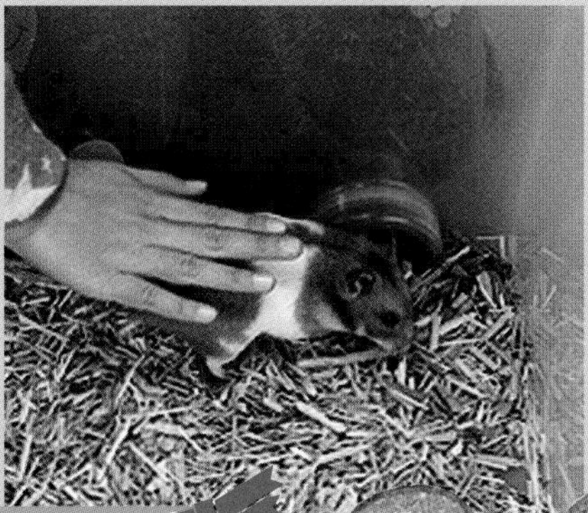

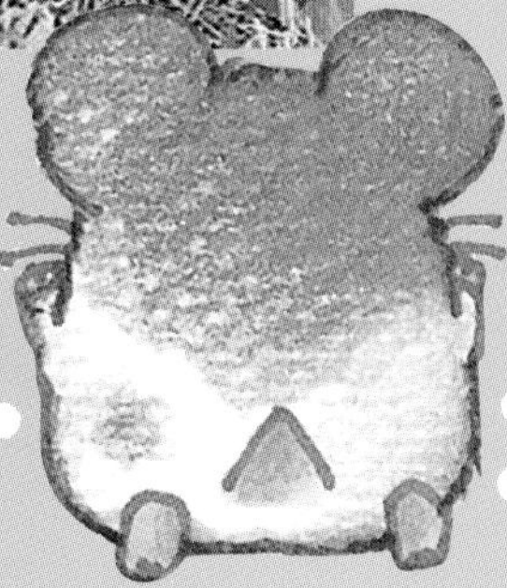

CHECKPOINTS

Happy: Gentle petting is very soothing.

Unhappy: It does not like to be touched when it is sleeping.

HOLD IT IN THE PALM OF YOUR HANDS. STEP 4

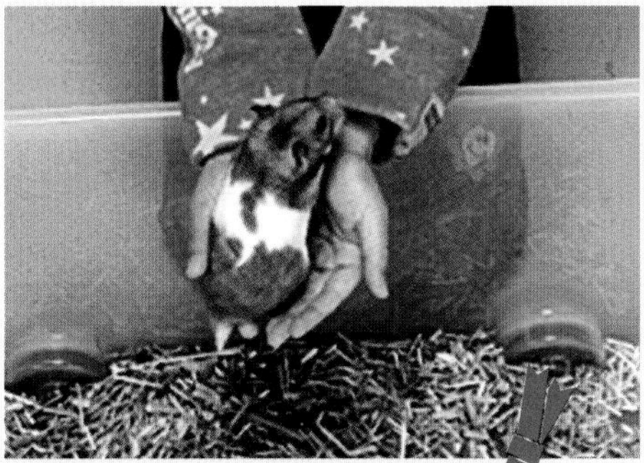

Hold your hamster by keeping your hands in a scooping position. Hamsters don't like high places, so make sure you are sitting down before handling your hamster.

CHECKPOINTS

Happy: If feels reassured when it is held while you are sitting.

Unhappy: It gets hurt when you hold it in a tight grip.

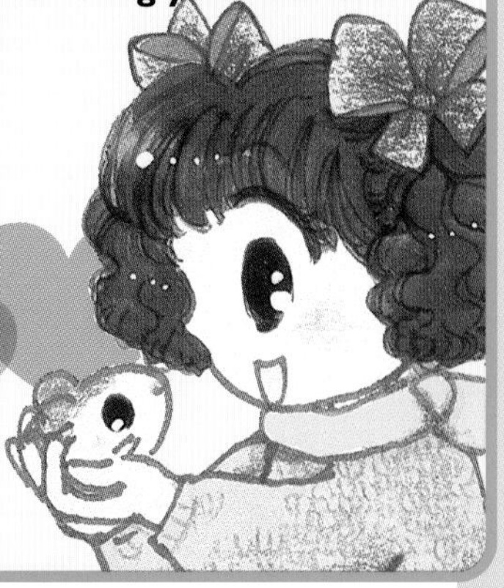

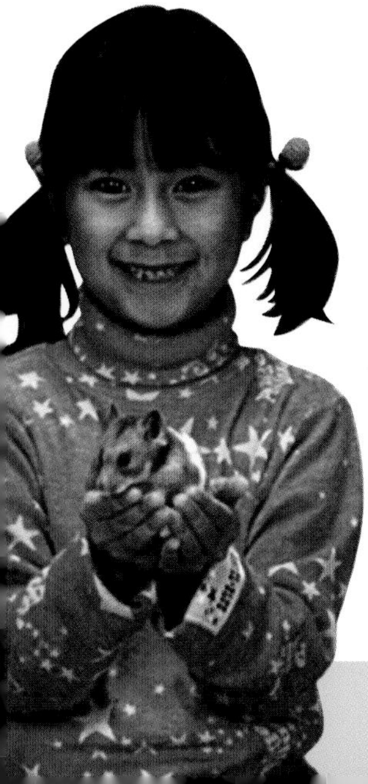

HOW TO BECOME HAMSTER-FRIENDLY

 WHEN A HAMSTER FIRST ARRIVES

It is natural to want to play with the hamster right away when it first arrives in your home. However, since the hamster has not gotten used to its new environment yet, this might cause the hamster to become stressed, and possibly ill.

For the first two or three days, quietly give it food and just watch over it. Clean up after the hamster and let it become reassured by its own scent building up in its cage. After making sure that it has gotten used to its new surroundings, gradually increase interaction.

 ESTABLISHING CONTACT WITH YOUR HAMSTER

In most cases, Golden Hamsters and Siberian Hamsters will get comfortable with you very quickly. However, some hamsters are neurotic or quick to anger, and have a very hard time adjusting. (Do not force yourself to keep such a hamster. Its life expectancy might be shortened due to stress. It might also bite people.)

However, the hamster does need to be moved when its cage is being cleaned. If you are unable to handle the hamster because it bites or dashes around to escape, capture it using a plastic box or tube. Be careful not to hurt it!

So as not to stress your hamster, please follow these rules:

- Do not grab it by its ears or tail. Do not squeeze when you hold it.
- Do not touch it suddenly.
- Do not place a collar or leash on your hamster.
- Do not let it play with dogs or cats.
- Do not put it in a bath.

Please take care not to scare the hamster in other ways. Hamsters are very small creatures and so become stressed at the slightest thing.

Suddenly waking a hamster who is sleeping deeply will scare it.

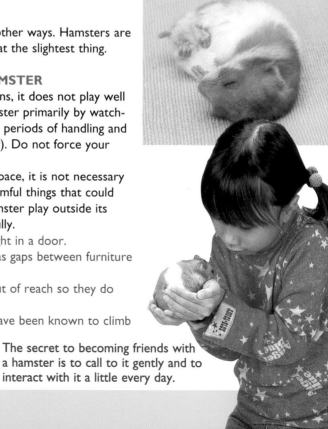

 HOW TO PLAY WITH YOUR HAMSTER

Even if a hamster is comfortable around humans, it does not play well for extended periods of time. Enjoy your hamster primarily by watching it play and move around in its home. Keep periods of handling and petting to a minimum (about 30 minutes a day). Do not force your hamster to play when it is scared or tired.

As long as your hamster's home has enough space, it is not necessary to let it play outside of it. There are many harmful things that could happen if it is released. If you must let the hamster play outside its cage, please note the following pointers carefully.

- Be careful it does not get stepped on or caught in a door.
- Cover all spaces that it might run into, such as gaps between furniture or other narrow spaces.
- Keep electrical cords and telephone cords out of reach so they do not get nibbled on.
- Don't let it climb to high places—hamsters have been known to climb up curtains.
- When a hamster is loose, don't let it run free in the home.

The secret to becoming friends with a hamster is to call to it gently and to interact with it a little every day.

46

CHAPTER 5 • A HAMSTER'S BODY

A HAMSTER'S BODY IS DIFFERENT FROM OUR HUMAN BODIES. CHECK ON IT DAILY SO THAT IT CAN STAY HEALTHY.

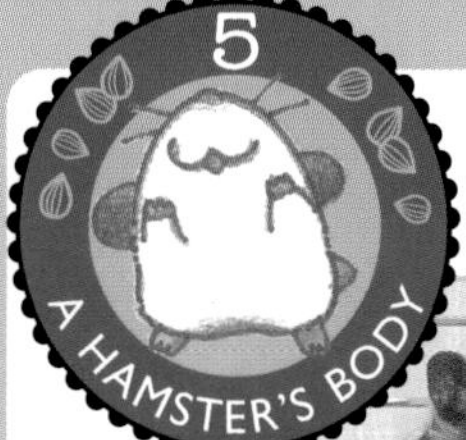
5
A HAMSTER'S BODY

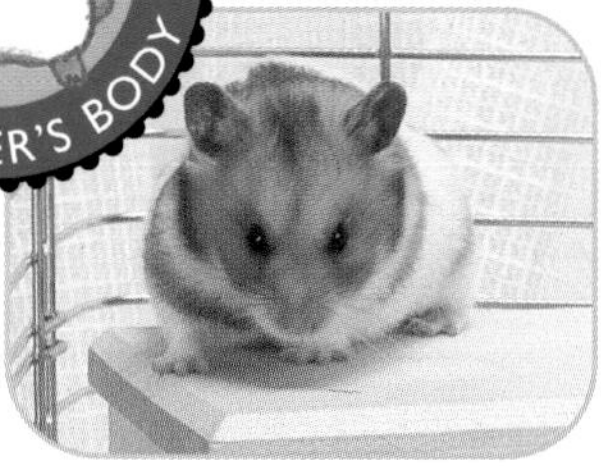

THE SECRETS OF A HAMSTER'S BODY

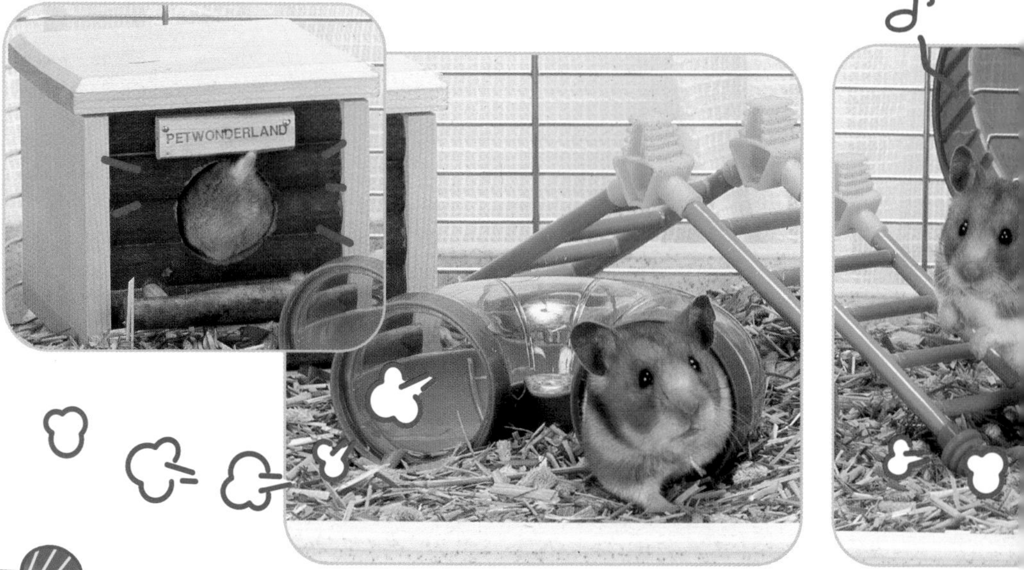
PETWONDERLAND

SECRET 1 Paws that can grab anything.

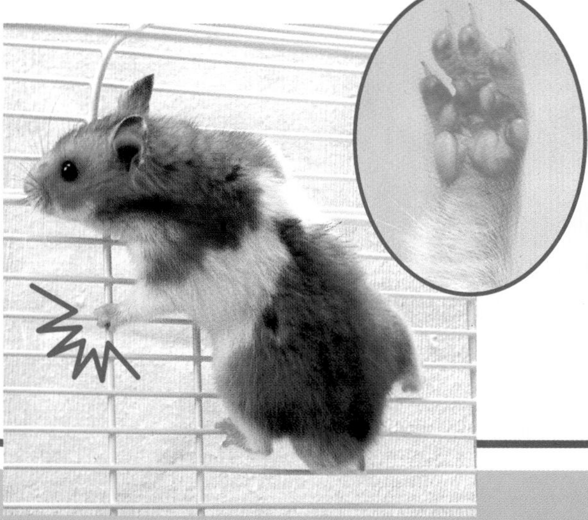

It can use its thin fingers to climb, but don't let it! hamsters aren't very good with heights.

Be careful it does not fall and hurt itself.

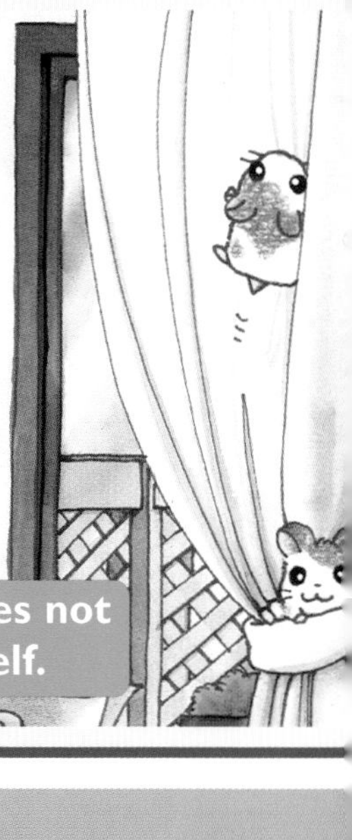

A hamster's body is full of surprises. It enables a hamster to explore lots of places.

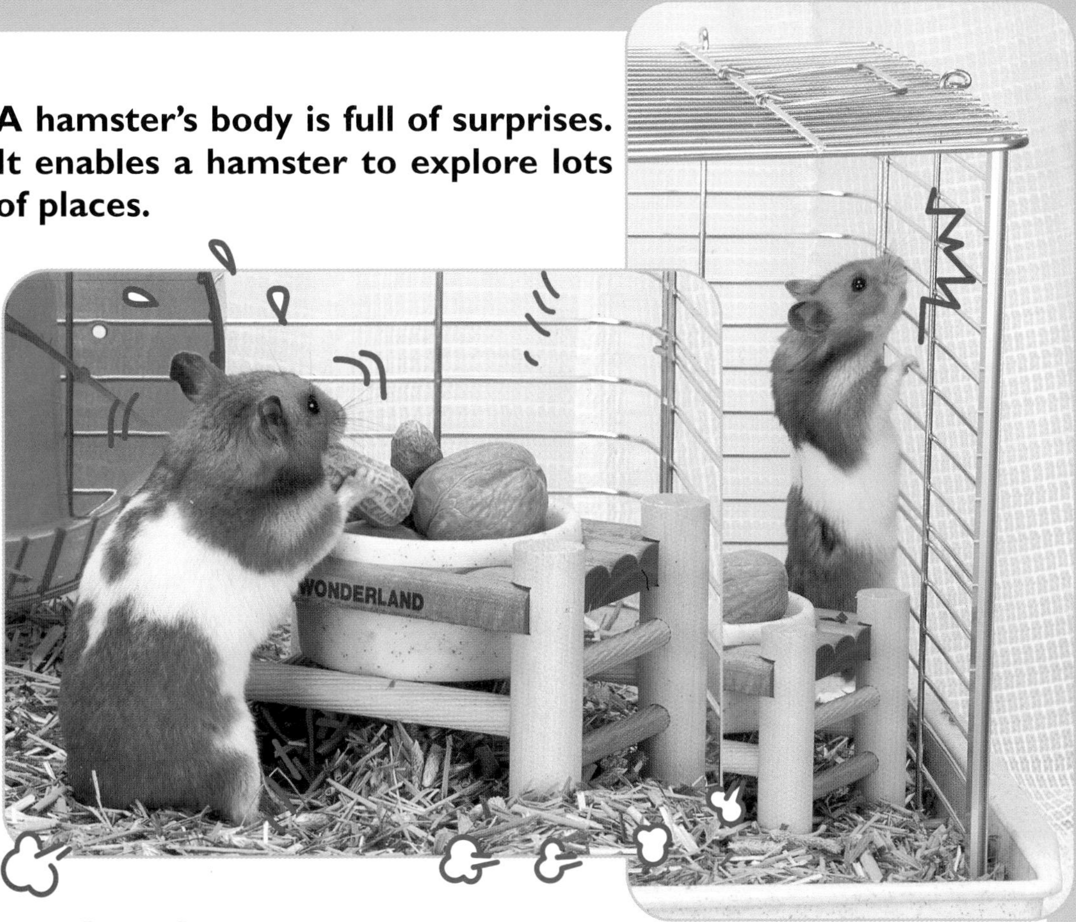
WONDERLAND

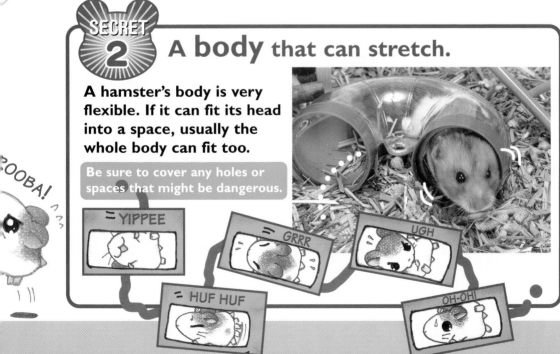

SECRET 2 A body that can stretch.

A hamster's body is very flexible. If it can fit its head into a space, usually the whole body can fit too.

Be sure to cover any holes or spaces that might be dangerous.

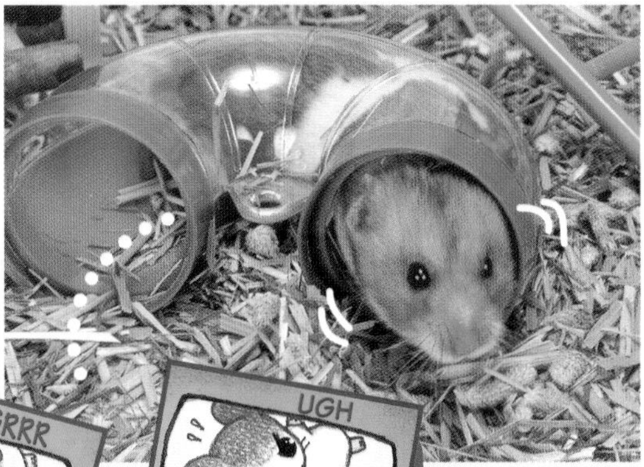

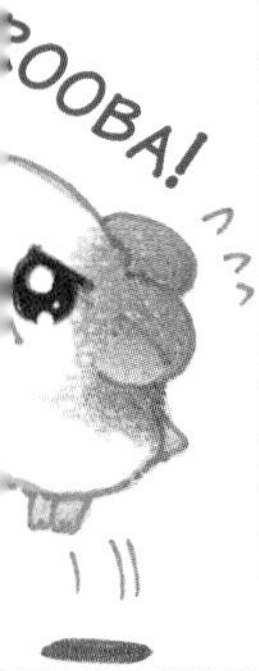

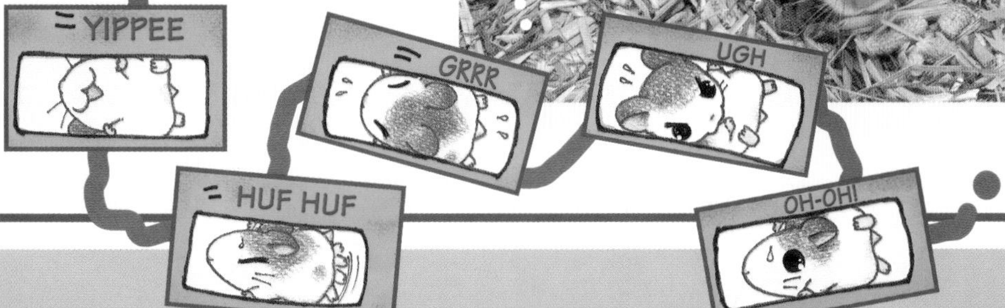
YIPPEE
HUF HUF
GRRR
UGH
OH-OH!

SECRET 3 Eyes that can see in the dark.

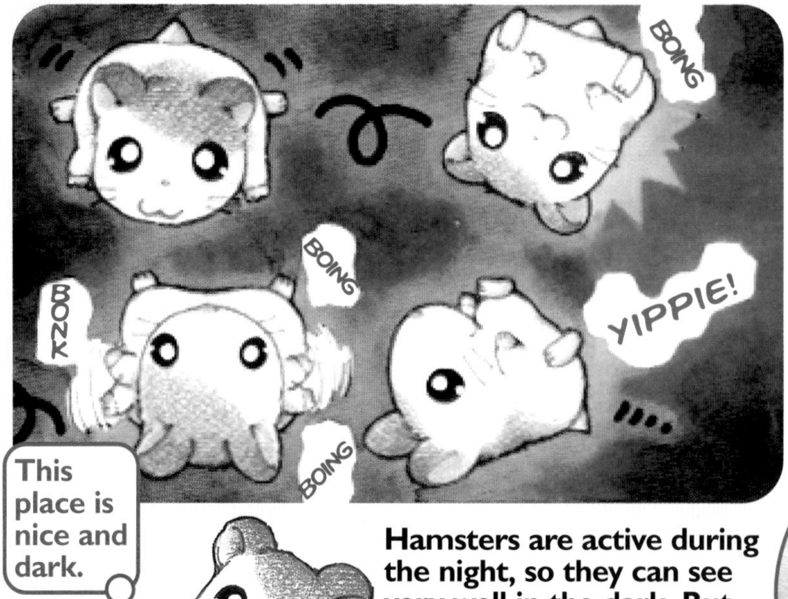
BOING
BOING
BONK
YIPPIE!
BOING
This place is nice and dark.

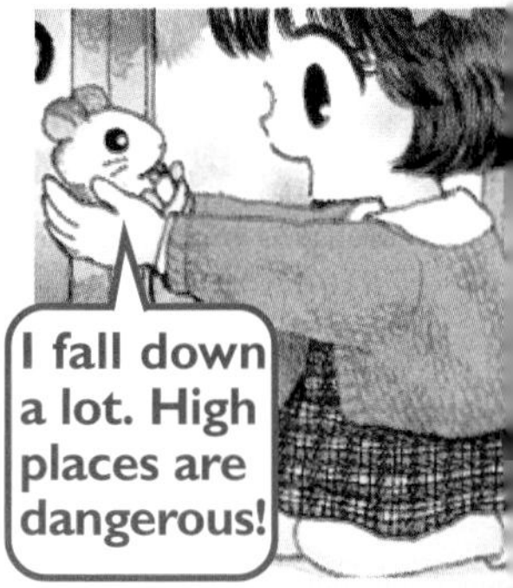
I fall down a lot. High places are dangerous!

Sit down when playing with your hamster.

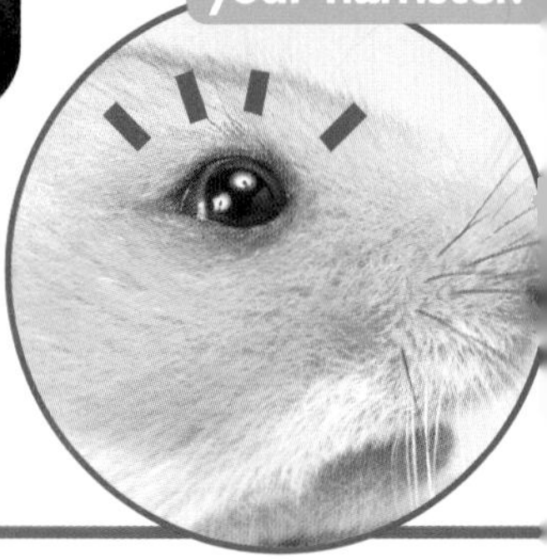

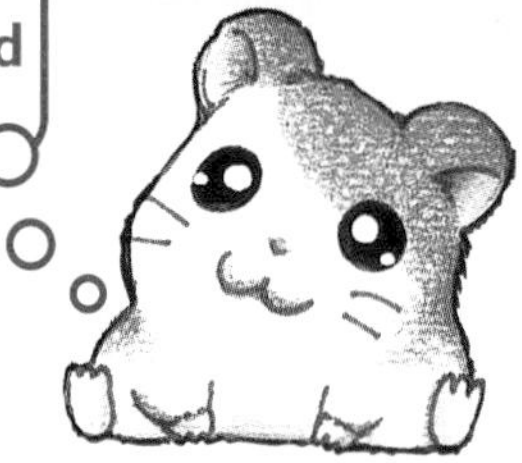

Hamsters are active during the night, so they can see very well in the dark. But they can't tell high places from low places, so they often fall.

SECRET 4 Ears that can hear the slightest noise.

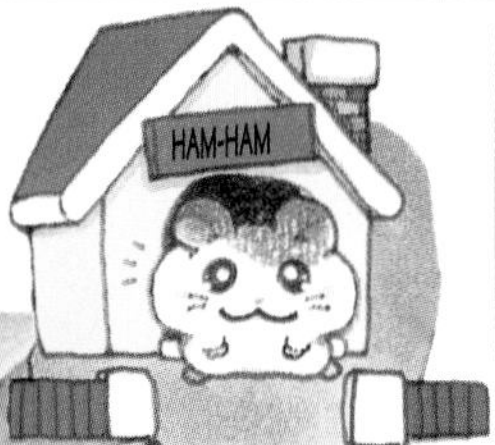
HAM-HAM

Try to keep the noise down as much as possibl around your hamster.

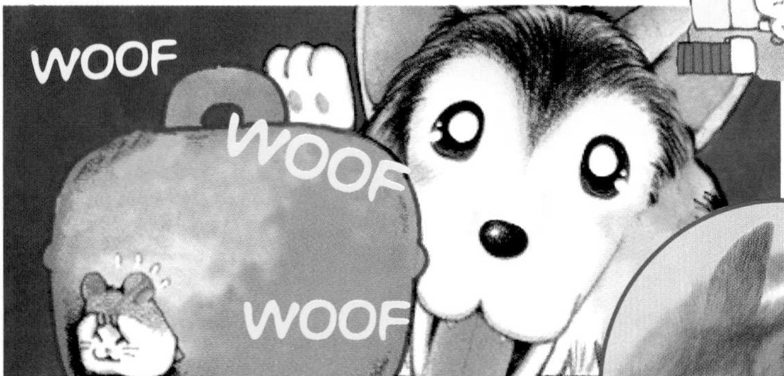
WOOF
WOOF
WOOF

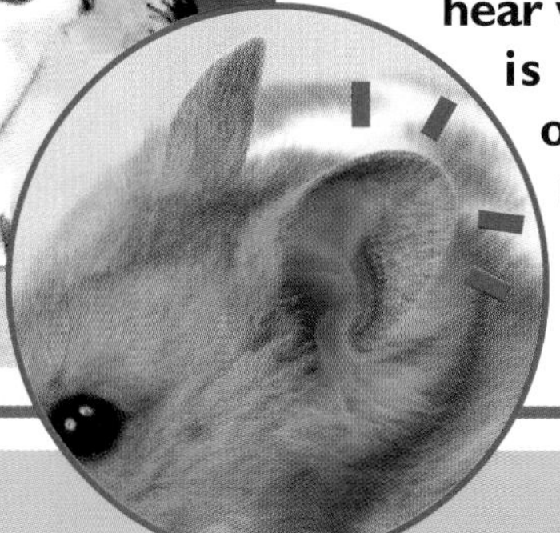

Hamsters' ears are very sensitive so that they ca hear when an enen is creeping up on them. Loud noises scare them a lot.

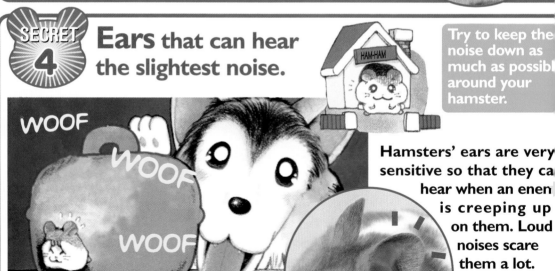

SECRET 5 Teeth that keep growing.

lamsters' teeth never stop rowing. They grind their eeth down by gnawing n hard things.

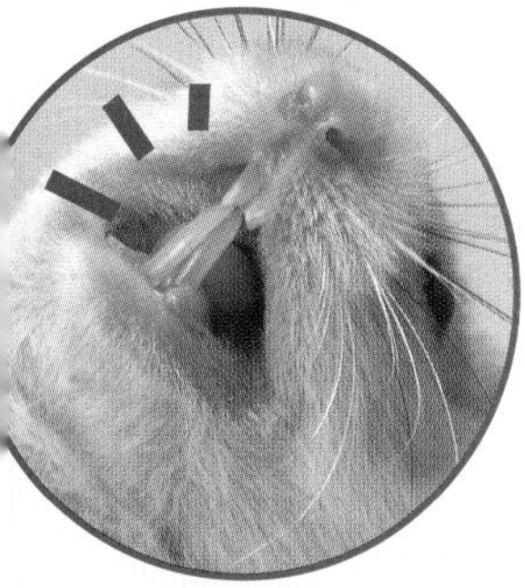

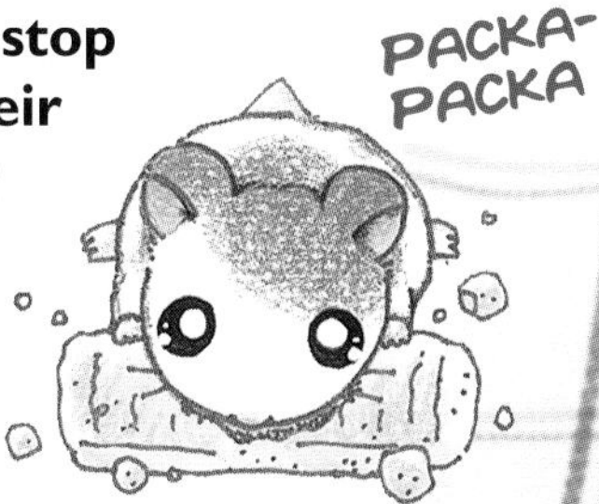
PACKA-
PACKA

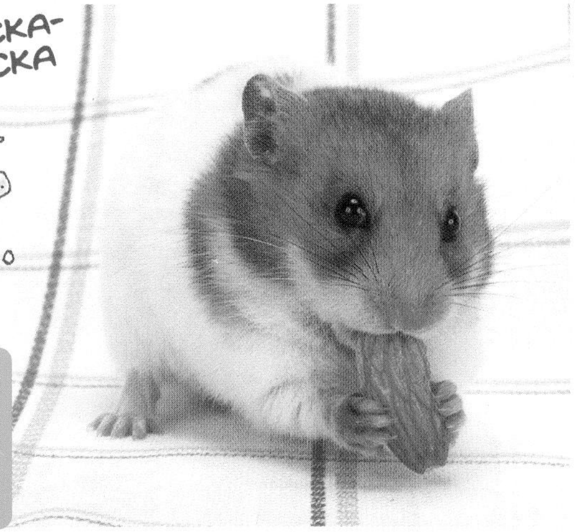

It's a good idea to give your hamster a hard-shelled nut once in a while.

SECRET 6 Cheek pouches to store and transport food.

lamsters' cheeks have a pouch for storing food. 'hey snack on this food later while adventuring.

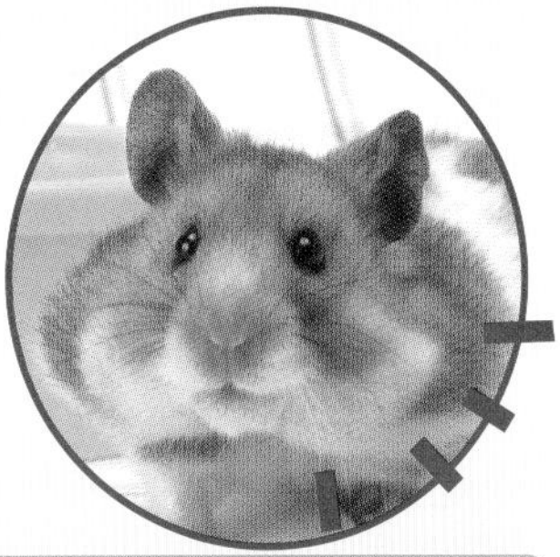

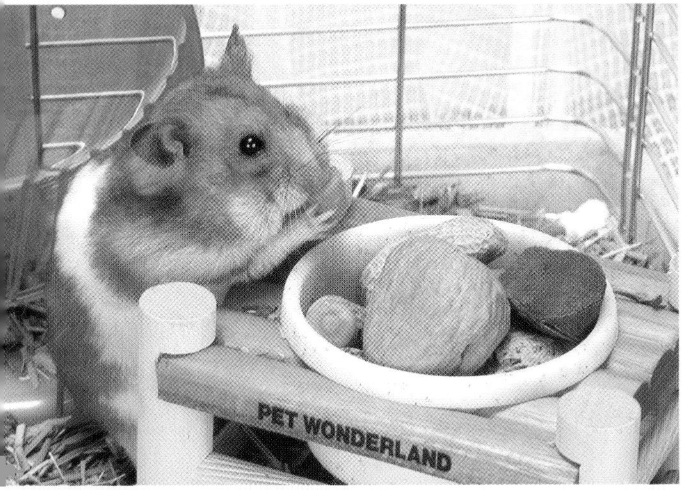
PET WONDERLAND

Do not give your hamster foods that melt in the mouth because they can spoil in a hamster's cheek pouches. If your hamster likes to store wet foods in its cheeks, give them only as a rare treat.

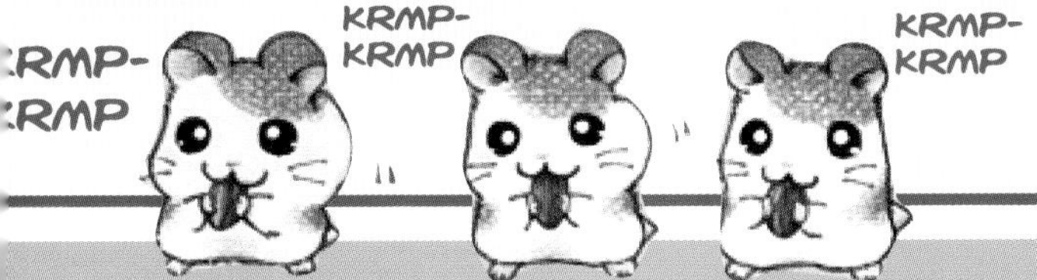
KRMP-
KRMP
KRMP-
KRMP
KRMP-
KRMP

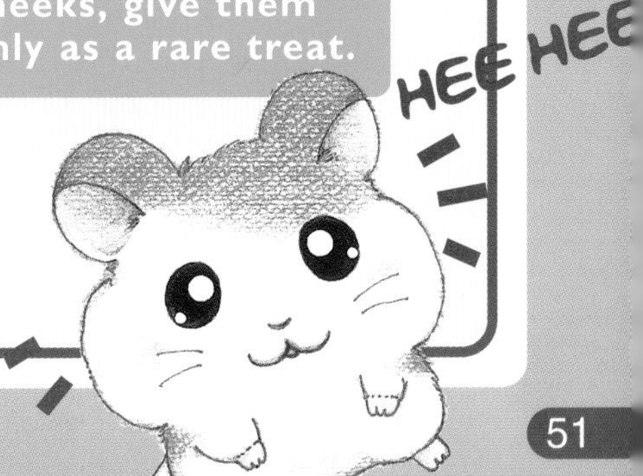
HEE HEE

PROTECTING YOUR HAMSTER FROM SICKNESS

A HAMSTER'S HEALTH CHECK-UP

Observe your hamster every day and check up on its health.

5
A HAMSTER'S BODY

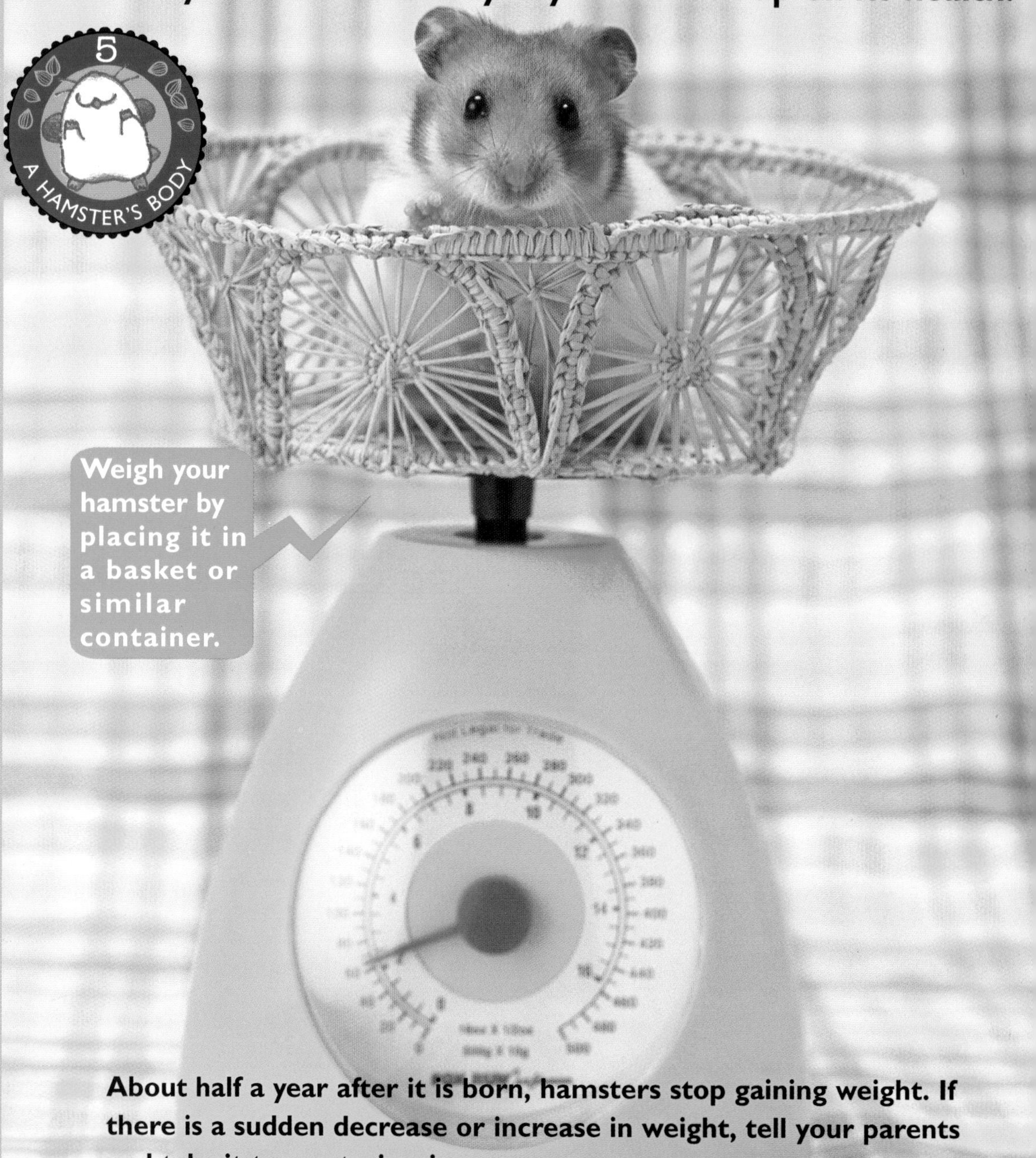

Weigh your hamster by placing it in a basket or similar container.

About half a year after it is born, hamsters stop gaining weight. If there is a sudden decrease or increase in weight, tell your parents and take it to a veterinarian.

A HAMSTER JOURNAL

DATE	WEATHER	TEMPERATURE
....	....	....

TODAY'S WEIGHT	ounces

TODAY'S MEAL	

TODAY'S CHORES	

CHECKPOINTS ✔

	FEEDING Is it eating well?			**EYES** No discharge from the eyes?	
	URINE Is it peeing regularly?			**NOSE** No discharge from the nose?	
	PLAYING Is it playing energetically?			**EARS** Are they pointing straight up?	
	BOTTOM No diarrhea?			**FUR** No bald spots?	

Copy this page for your hamster journal. Place a ✔ in the box if the answer to the question is "yes." If several squares have no ✔ marks, tell your parents. Your hamster may need to see a veterinarian.

HOW TO PROTECT THE HEALTH OF YOUR HAMSTER

HOW TO GET THROUGH WINTERS AND SUMMERS

Hamsters do not do too well in either cold or hot weather. As much as possible, keep the temperature between 68~71.6°F (20~22°C).

WINTER

When the weather gets cold, place the cage in a warm room and provide plenty of bedding. You can also surround the cage with cardboard, but make sure the airflow isn't obstructed, and don't let it get too hot. Hamsters like temperatures similar to what people like, only a little warmer. And remember, your hamster needs air to breathe, just like you do! Golden Hamsters are known to go into hibernation if it gets too cold. During hibernation, hamsters lower their body temperature to below 50°F (10°C). Since bringing their body temperature back up to normal requires a lot of energy, there are instances when they cannot wake up on their own. If your hamster goes into hibernation, wake your hamster slowly by gradually raising the room temperature. To prevent hibernation from happening, make sure that the hamster is kept warm.

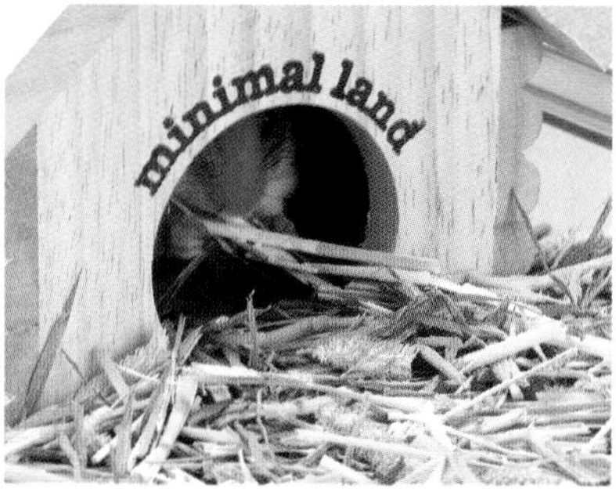
minimal land
When it gets cold, make sure that plenty of nesting material is available. The hamster will bring it into its house on its own.

SUMMER

Hamsters can succumb to heat stroke if kept in a hot and poorly ventilated room. Keep your hamster's room cool by using air conditioners or fans (make sure that the breeze does not blow directly onto the hamster).

If possible, place the hamster in a breezy cage during the summer (but safe from cats) and in a well-insulated, cloth-covered cage during the winter. Make sure the hamster can't reach the cloth to chew on it, as this may injure your hamster.

HAMSTER SICKNESSES

Like humans, hamsters can come down with a variety of diseases. With such a small creature as a hamster, by the time you suspect something is wrong, the sickness might have progressed to a dangerous stage. If you see any of the following symptoms, take your hamster to an animal hospital as soon as possible.

DIARRHEA

Because hamsters have such small bodies, they can become dehydrated very quickly, so diarrhea can be life-threatening.

BLOOD COMING OUT OF ITS REPRODUCTIVE ORGANS

Hamsters do not have menstrual cycles. Any bloody discharge is clearly abnormal.

GROWTHS ON THE BODY

There is a possibility that it may be cancer.

OVERGROWN TEETH

If its front teeth get too long and its bite does not match, your hamster will find it hard to eat and it might injure the inside of its mouth. Take it to the animal hospital to get its teeth trimmed. Get your pet a chew tree from the pet store to prevent this.

There are many other illnesses that can potentially afflict your hamster. Be sure to find out where the animal hospital nearest to your home is in case your hamster needs medical attention at any time.

TRANSMISSION OF INFECTION TO HUMANS

The transfer of illness from animal to human is called "zoonosis." As long as proper care and hygiene are maintained, there is little probability of getting a disease from your pet hamster. In order to provide a safe environment, note the following:

- Clean up after your hamster every day.
- Wash your hands with antibacterial soap before and after handling your hamster.
- Do not snack while caring for or playing with your hamster.
- Do not kiss your hamster.
- Do not feed your hamster treats mouth-to-mouth.
- Do not give your hamster table scraps.

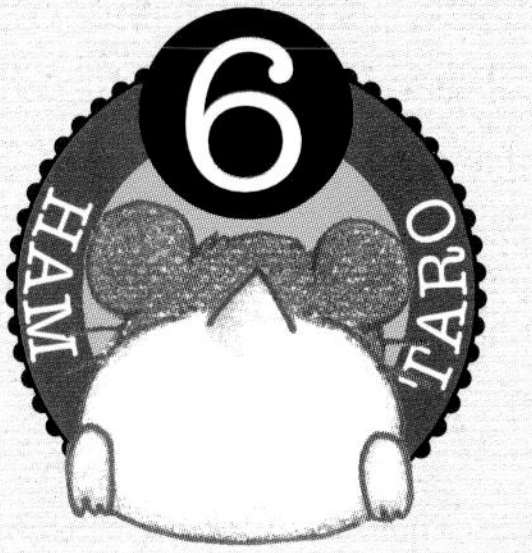
6
HAM
TARO

CHAPTER 6 • BABY HAMSTERS

BABY HAMSTERS ARE TINY AND CUTE.
WATCH THEM GROW UP!

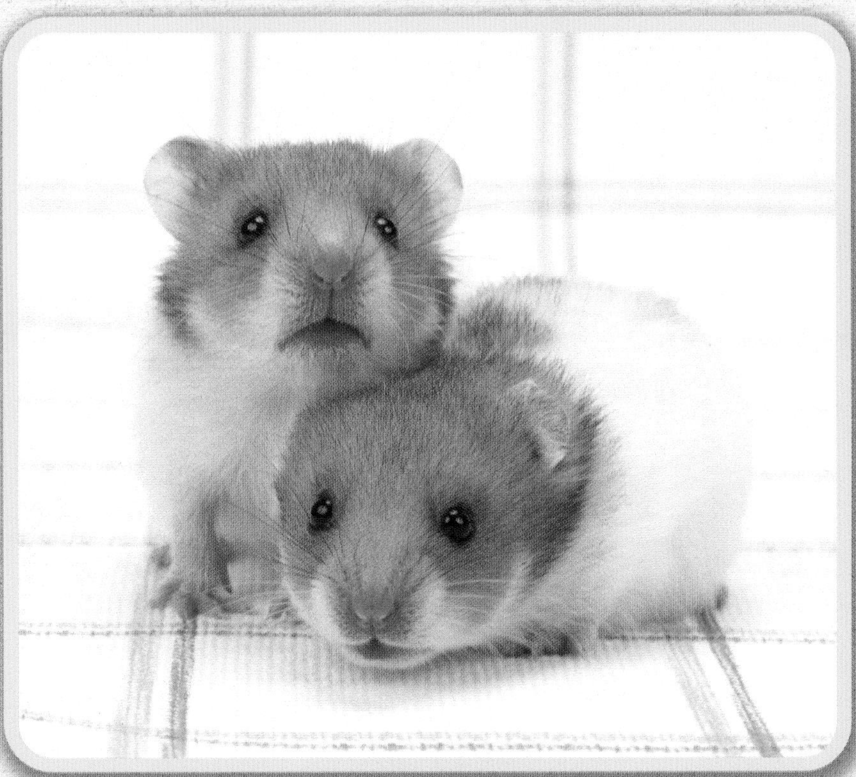

6
BABY HAMSTERS

WARNING!!

Hamsters produce many babies each pregnancy—as many as 17! Talk it over with your family before breeding hamsters to see if you are able to care for so many.

Bring together a healthy male and female more than three months old.

When you have the two together in one cage, keep a close eye on both hamsters. If they start to fight, separate them right away.

STEP 1

THE FIRST MEETING

Place their cages next to each other for their first meeting. If they sniff each other, move on to step 2!

HIF-HIF HIF-HI

STEP 2

FRIENDS

Place the female in the cage of the male. If they sniff each other, this means that they want to be friends. If they continue to be friends and do not fight, leave them together in the cage for approximately 7 days. After this time, separate the hamsters.

A ROMANTIC WEDDING
NEWLYWED ♥ HAMSTERS

Have a hamster wedding, and invite your whole family!

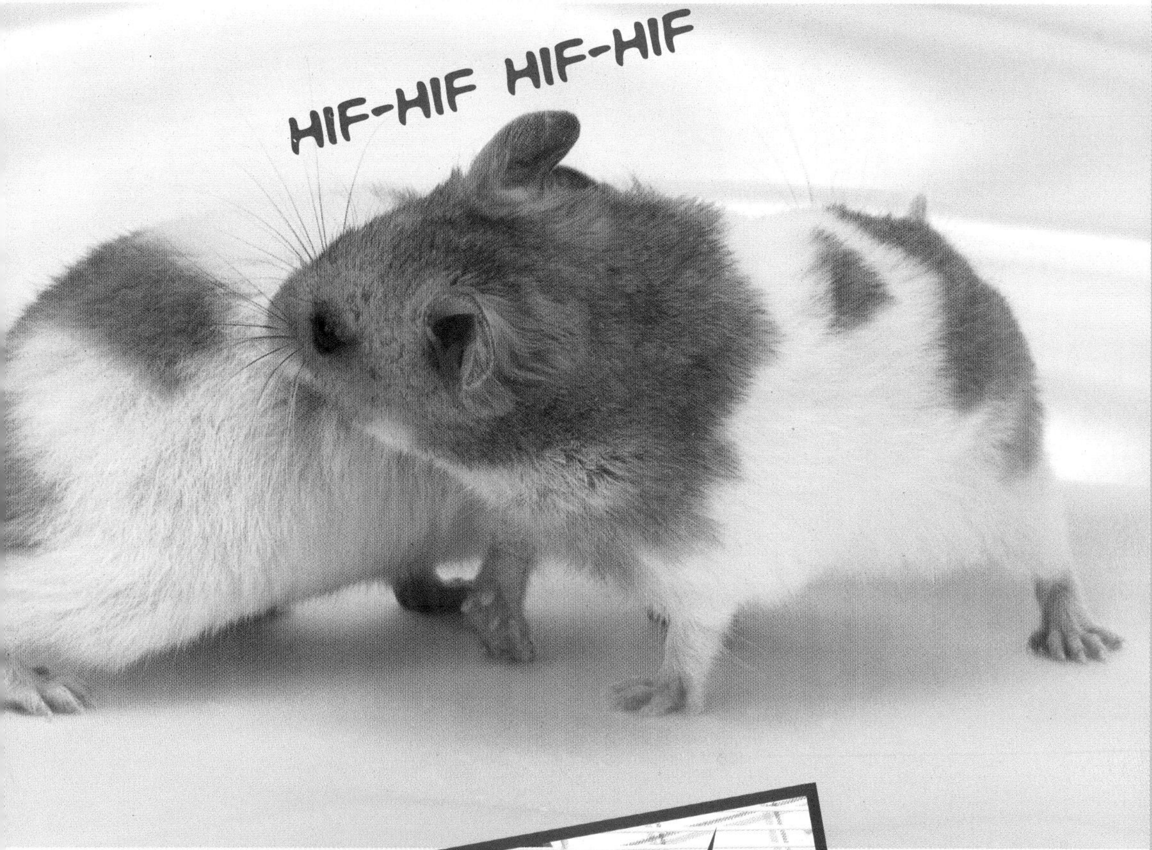
HIF-HIF HIF-HIF

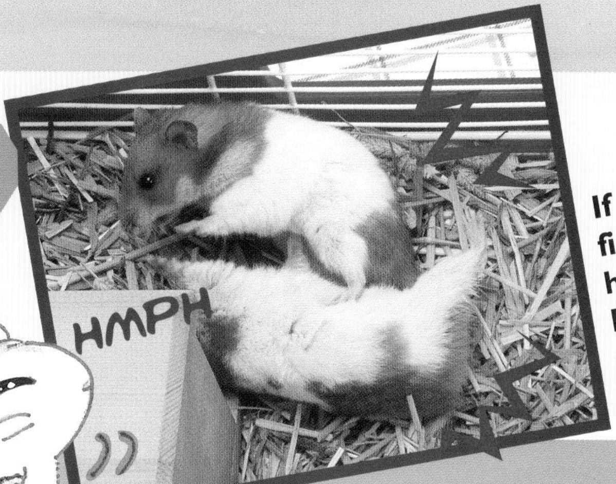
HMPH

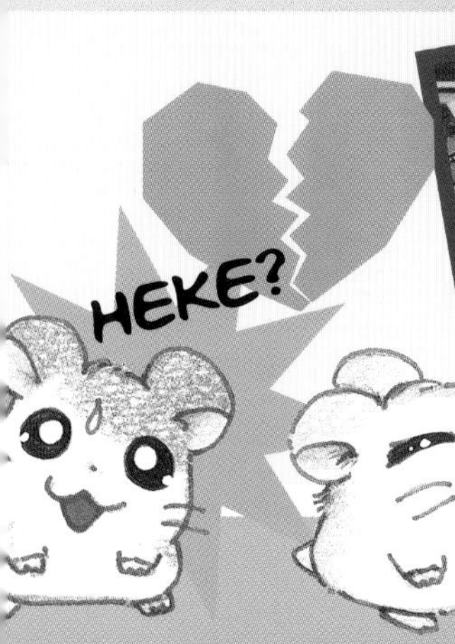
HEKE?

If they start to fight, the marriage has failed. Immediately separate the hamsters!

6

BABY HAMSTERS

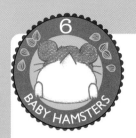

LOTS OF BABIES

NURSING HAMSTERS

Since so many babies are born, the mother hamster is constantly busy.

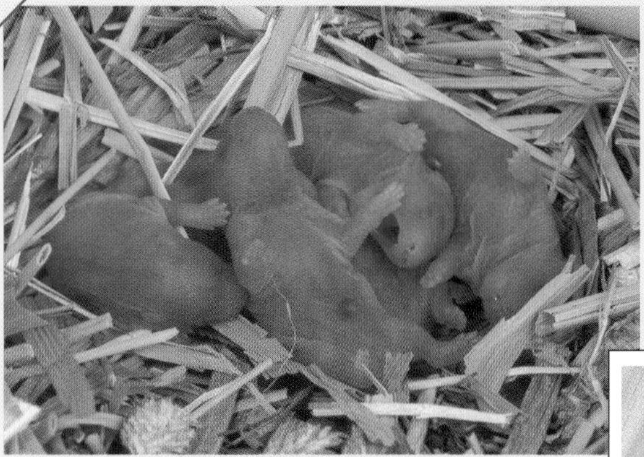

DAY ONE

THE BABIES ARE BORN!

Newborn hamsters have no hair.

At birth a baby hamster weigh only a few grams.

The mother hamster warms the babies with her body heat.

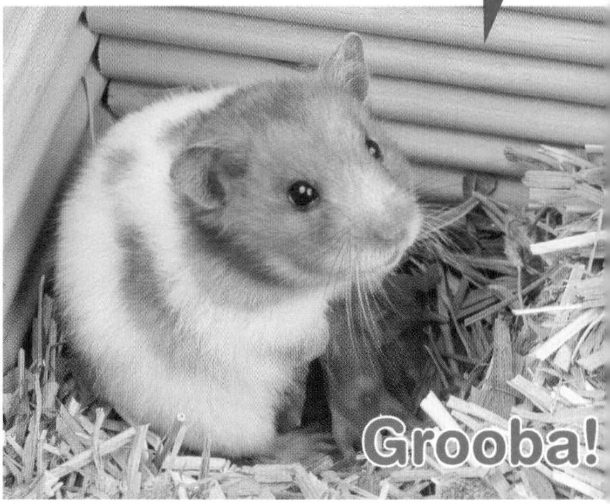
Grooba!

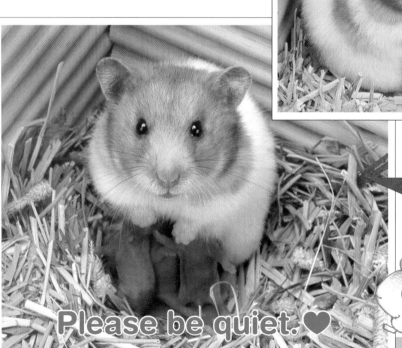

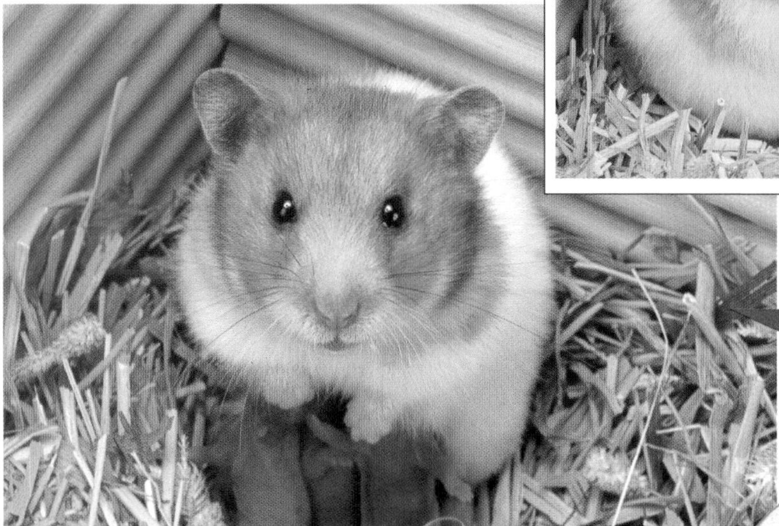
Please be quiet.♥

The mother hamste is busy raising her children. Watch ove them quietly and do not bother them.

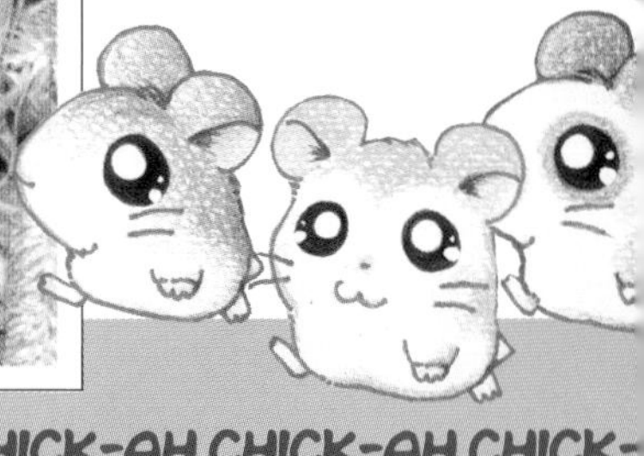

CHICK-AH CHICK-AH CHICK-

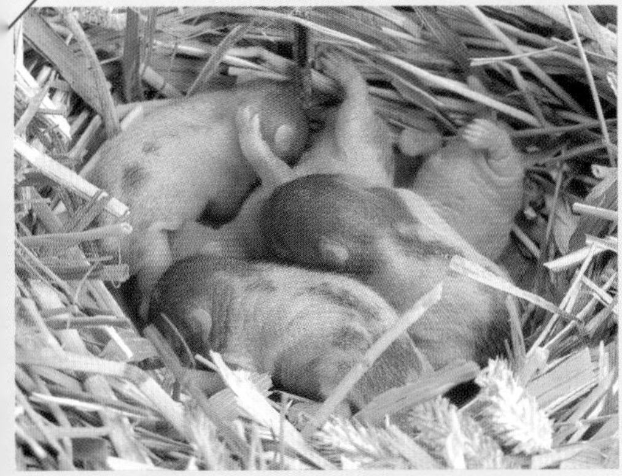

DAY FIVE

THE BABIES' EARS ARE BEGINNING TO TAKE SHAPE.

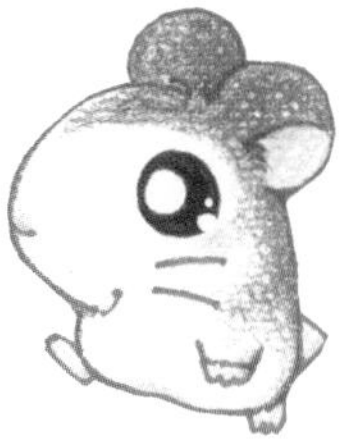

The babies' ears, which were just bumps when they were born, are now shaped more like their mother's.

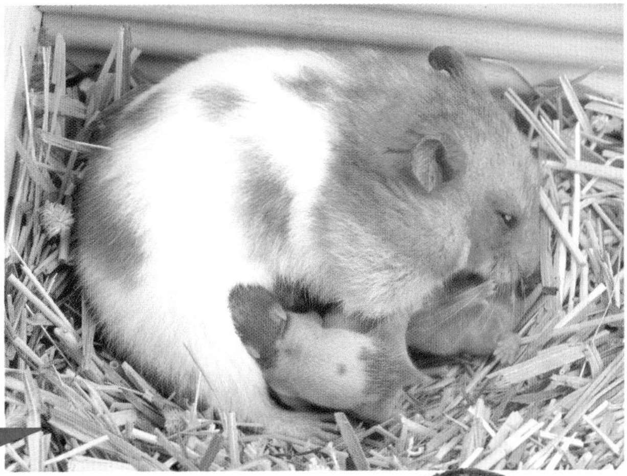

The mother hamster cleans her babies by licking their bottoms.

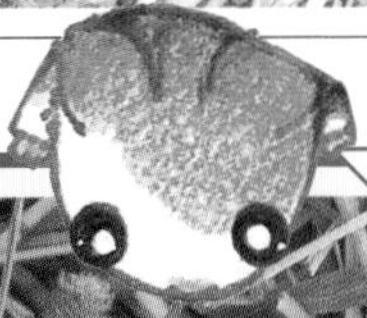

DAY EIGHT

THE BABIES' BODIES ARE NOW COVERED WITH HAIR.

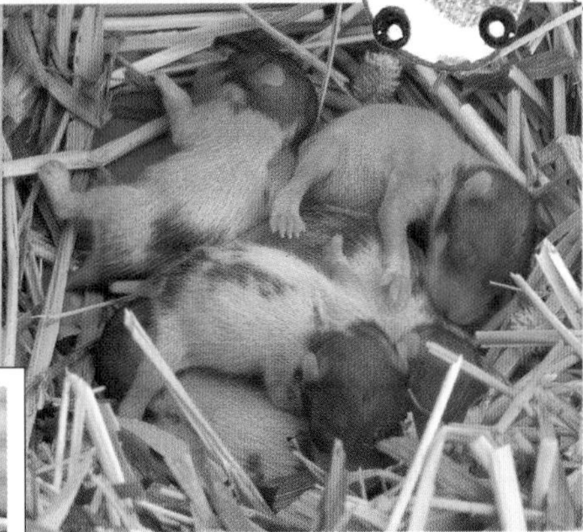

Dark hairs will grow out of the dark areas.

When the mother hamster moves, the babies, still sucking on her nipples, are dragged along with her.

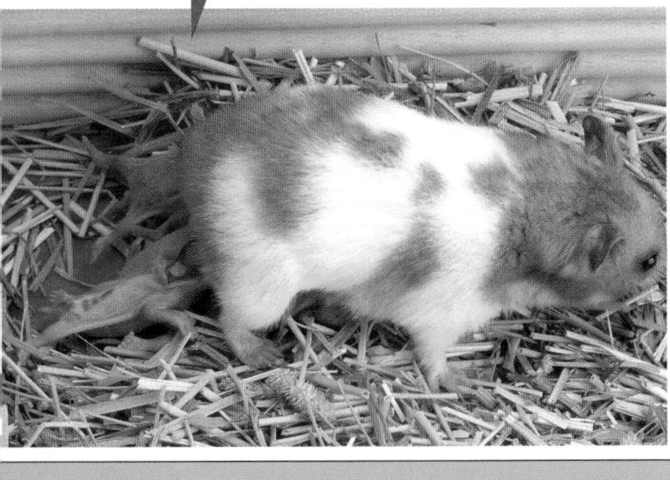

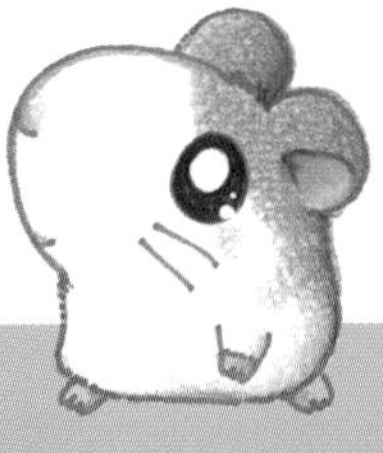

6 BABY HAMSTERS

GOING SOLO IN 21 DAYS
GROWING HAMSTERS

Hamsters grow quickly, and in just 21 days are able to live on their own.

The energetic babies like to wander around. The mother hamster gather them all by gently picking them up in her mouth.

DAY TEN
....

THE BABIES CAN EAT SOLID FOODS.

The babies can now eat the same foods as their mother. But still, they seem to like their mother's milk better.

TICKY-TICKY

DAY FIFTEEN
....

THE BABIES OPEN THEIR EYES.

The eyes, which have been closed since birth, finally open.

Yum Yum

Practicing getting food out of the feeder.

DAY EIGHTEEN

ALMOST BIG ENOUGH TO GO SOLO.

Kushi-Kushi

Kushi-Kushi

PRACTICING GROOMING

DAY TWENTY-ONE TO THIRTY

GOOD-BYE, MOM

The baby hamsters can live on their own. They no longer have to drink milk, and can do everything by themselves. (The smaller varieties may take up to a month to wean.) Keep each of the young hamsters in a separate cage. If you keep them together, they will fight each other.

TIPS ON BREEDING HAMSTERS

BEFORE BREEDING HAMSTERS

Hamster babies can be very cute, but it is possible for a hamster to have up to 20 babies at a time, and as soon as they can live on their own, they will each need their own cage! Due to the space necessary for the hamsters and the time needed to care for each, this will greatly increase the work and stress of caring for them. Make sure to have other homes ready before breeding your hamster.

HOW TO BREED YOUR HAMSTER

Breeding should only be allowed under close adult supervision.

Although hamsters can biologically start breeding from 2 months of age, their bodies have not fully matured yet. Breeding hamsters should be between the ages of 3 months and 1 year. Make sure that both the male and the female hamster are healthy and that they are not related.

Females become fertile in 4-day cycles. Males are continuously fertile once they mature. If the female hamster's fertile day falls on the day that they are placed together, the male and female might cross tails and fertilization may occur immediately. When a female in heat comes near a male, she arches up her back and raises her tail to tell a male that she is ready to breed.

Even if they are placed together after she is out of heat, a fertile day will arrive at least once during the week. Limit the time they are together to one week, even if they are not fighting. If she is pregnant, she will give birth in about 16 days (21 days for Siberian hamsters, up to 30 for the dwarf varieties). If, after one month, she does not give birth, start the process over again.

When the number of babies being carried is small, the mother hamster's belly might not be very noticeable, even though she is near to giving birth. After the hamsters meet, care for the female with the possibility of pregnancy in mind for about 20 days (one month for Siberian hamsters), and do not use the size of the belly as a marker.

The growth rate of baby hamsters varies. Use 21 days as a guideline and wean them off milk only after they can eat solids on their own.

CARING FOR A PREGNANT HAMSTER AND CARING FOR ITS YOUNG

CLEANING

Right before and after giving birth, the mother hamster is in a state of high alert. Once there is a possibility of a pregnancy, keep cleaning of the cage to a minimum and just discard very soiled nesting material. From the time the babies are born until they are able to be on their own, keep the cleaning of the cage to a minimum. However, be sure to keep a fresh supply of bedding available. The female will carry it by herself to the nest.

14 days after the birth, you may remove the mother from the cage and give it a thorough cleaning.

FOOD

A very nutritious diet and a plentiful supply of fresh water is extremely important for the growth of the babies while the mother hamster is pregnant, and for the production of rich milk after the birth of the babies.

Increase the amount of feed. It is not necessary to give the babies extra milk-based foods.

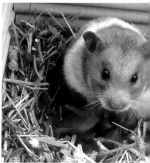

During pregnancy and child-rearing provide food and water without upsetting the mother hamster.

INTERACTION

It is possible for the mother hamster to stop caring for her young if she is placed in an environment where she does not feel safe.

Refrain from touching the babies or from peeking into the nest. Create a quiet environment so the mother hamster can feel calm and comfortable while raising her babies.

If a baby has strayed from the nest and the mother hamster has not noticed, return the baby to the nest before its body temperature drops. Do not touch the baby hamster directly. Instead, use a clean object, like a plastic spoon, to scoop up and gently move the baby.

THANK YOU FOR
READING THIS BOOK
ALL THE WAY
THROUGH.
I'M GLAD
WE'RE FRIENDS!

HAMSTER CARE GUIDE

Japanese Edition

Illustrations/Ritsuko Kawai
Text/Mizue Ono
Photography/Hideyuki Asakura
Editors/Yoko Nakase, Tatsushi Hosokawa

English Edition

Translation/Kaori Kawakubo
Editor/Lance Caselman
Cover & Graphic Design/Sean Lee
U.S. Veterinary Consultant/Dr. Joanne Howl
Production Coordinator/Masumi Washington

Managing Editor/Annette Roman
Vice-President of Sales & Marketing/Rick Bauer
Vice-President of Editorial/Hyoe Narita
Publisher/Seiji Horibuchi

Printed in Canada.

Published by Viz Communications, Inc.
P.O. Box 77010
San Francisco, CA 94107

10 9 8 7 6 5 4 3 2 1
First printing, October, 2002

To order Hamtaro books, visit www.hamtaro.com
or call us toll free at (800) 394-3042!

WWW.VIZKIDS.COM